"I Came Back to the Institute to Join You."

Kaitlyn's heart was pounding with the risk. "You have to believe me, Gabriel." This was it, the time to see whether she was going to make it as a spy. She stepped closer to Gabriel. "Test me."

If he wanted, he could reach into her mind and rip the truth out. Her thin shields wouldn't hold against him.

But he didn't try to probe her brain. He kissed her instead.

Kaitlyn surrendered to the kiss deliberately, and she felt a flash of triumph. Then the triumph was swept away by something much stronger and deeper. Something fierce and joyous—and *pure*.

Electricity seemed to arc between them. Everywhere they touched Kaitlyn could feel the sparks. They were together, *together,* so close, and she wanted to be closer. To join minds with him.

The ultimate sharing—but she *couldn't*. She would have no shields—he would see the truth and know that she'd come to the Institute as a spy.

Kaitlyn tried to pull away . . . but it didn't work.

Books by L. J. SMITH

THE FORBIDDEN GAME, VOLUME I: THE HUNTER
THE FORBIDDEN GAME, VOLUME II: THE CHASE
THE FORBIDDEN GAME, VOLUME III: THE KILL
DARK VISIONS: VOLUME I: THE STRANGE POWER
DARK VISIONS: VOLUME II: THE POSSESSED
DARK VISIONS: VOLUME III: THE PASSION
NIGHT WORLD: SECRET VAMPIRE
NIGHT WORLD: DAUGHTERS OF DARKNESS
NIGHT WORLD: SPELLBINDER
NIGHT WORLD: DARK ANGEL
NIGHT WORLD: THE CHOSEN
NIGHT WORLD: SOULMATE

Available from ARCHWAY Paperbacks

Volume III

L.J.SMITH

AN ARCHWAY PAPERBACK
Published by POCKET BOOKS
New York   London   Toronto   Sydney   Tokyo   Singapore

AN ARCHWAY PAPERBACK *Original*

An Archway Paperback published by
POCKET BOOKS, a division of Simon & Schuster Inc.
1230 Avenue of the Americas, New York, NY 10020

Copyright © 1995 by Lisa J. Smith

ISBN: 0-671-87456-X

First Archway Paperback printing April 1995

10 9 8 7 6 5 4 3 2

AN ARCHWAY PAPERBACK and colophon are registered trademarks of Simon & Schuster Inc.

Cover art by Danilo Ducak

Printed in the U.S.A

IL 7+

For Pat MacDonald, editor extraordinaire, whose keen insight helped shape my visions, and whose boundless patience allowed me to perfect them.

1

A dog barked, shattering the midnight silence. Gabriel glanced up briefly, his psychic senses alert. Then he went back to breaking into the house.

In a moment, the lock on the door gave way to his lockpick. The door swung open.

Gabriel smiled.

There were four people awake in the house. One of them Kaitlyn. Beautiful Kaitlyn with the red-gold hair. A pity he might have to destroy her—but he was her enemy from now on. He couldn't afford weakness.

He was working for Mr. Zetes now. And Mr. Zetes needed something—a shard from the last perfect crystal in the world. Kaitlyn had it . . . Gabriel was going to take it.

As simple as that.

If anyone tried to stop him, he was going to have to hurt them. Even Kaitlyn.

For just an instant there was a tightening in his

chest. Then his face hardened and he moved stealthily into the dark house.

"Give up, Kaitlyn."

Kaitlyn looked into Gabriel's dark gray eyes.

"How did you get *in* here?" she said.

Gabriel smiled silkily. "Breaking and entering is one of my new talents."

"This is Marisol's house," Rob said from behind him. "You can't just—"

"But I *have* just. Don't expect help; I've put everybody outside to sleep. I'm here, and I think you know why."

They all stared at him: Kaitlyn and Rob and Lewis and Anna. They were refugees, runaways from the Zetes Institute for Psychic Research, and Marisol's family had taken them in. Marisol herself was absent; once a research assistant at the Institute, she'd found out too much and ended up in a coma. But her family had been kind—and now Kaitlyn had brought more trouble on them.

It was past midnight. The four of them had been sitting up in the room Marisol's brother had assigned the girls, talking and trying to figure out what to do next. And then the door had opened to reveal Gabriel.

Kaitlyn, who was standing directly in front of the handsome mahogany desk by Marisol's bed, made her face utterly blank. She tried to make her mind blank, too.

Anna and Lewis, who were sitting on the bed, were looking just as blank, and Rob's mind was just one wash of golden light. Nothing for Gabriel to grab onto.

It didn't matter. He looked past Kaitlyn, at the desk, and his smile was dazzling and dangerous.

"Give up," he said again. "I want it, and I'm going to get it."

"We don't know what you're talking about," Rob said flatly, taking a step toward him.

Gabriel answered without turning to look at Rob. He was still smiling but his eyes were dark. "A shard of the last perfect crystal," he said. "Do you want to play hot and cold—or should I just take it?" He looked at the desk again.

"If we did have it, we wouldn't be giving it to you," Rob said. "We'd use it to destroy your boss—he is your boss now, isn't he?"

Gabriel's smile froze. His eyes narrowed slightly, and Kaitlyn could see darkness filling them. But his voice was calm and easygoing. "Sure, he's my boss. And you'd better stay away from him or you're going to get hurt."

Kaitlyn could feel a stinging behind her eyes. She didn't believe this was happening, she *didn't.* Gabriel was standing here like a stranger, warning them away from Mr. Zetes. From *Mr. Zetes,* the man who'd tried to make them into psychic weapons to sell to the highest bidder, who'd tried to kill them when they rebelled. Who'd hounded them all the way up to Canada when they ran away from him, and who was clearly still after them now that they'd returned to fight him. They'd hoped Marisol's house would be a safe place to hide from him—but they'd been wrong.

"How *can* you, Gabriel?" Anna said in her low, clear voice, and Kaitlyn knew she was feeling the same thing. Anna Eva Whiteraven's face—usually serene between its dark braids of hair—was now clouded. "How can you join him? After everything he's done—"

"—and everything he's going to do," Lewis put in. Lewis Chao was normally as cheerful as Anna was serene, but now his almond-shaped eyes were bleak.

"He's bad, Gabriel; he's bad, and you know it," Rob said, closing in from behind. Rob Kessler wasn't built for menace either, but just now with his tousled blond hair and blazing golden eyes he looked like an avenging angel.

"And he'll turn on *you* in the end," Kaitlyn said, adding her voice to the chorus against Gabriel. In her mind she added herself to the group: Kaitlyn Fairchild, not as gentle as Anna and Lewis or as good as Rob, a girl with fiery hair and a temper. And eyes that people called witchy, smoky blue with darker blue rings in them. Right now, Kait fixed these eyes mercilessly on Gabriel, staring him down.

Gabriel Wolfe threw back his head and laughed.

As always, it almost took Kaitlyn's breath away. Gabriel was so handsome it was frightening. His pale skin made his dark hair look even darker, like the silky pelt of some animal—like his namesake. A wolf, a predator in his bones, who enjoyed stalking and toying with his prey.

Of course he's bad, Gabriel said. Kaitlyn heard the words in her head, rather than with her ears, and the tone was amused and mocking. *I'm bad, too—or hadn't you noticed?*

Tiny needles of pain jabbed into Kaitlyn's temples.

She managed not to gasp, but she could sense Anna's alarm, and Lewis's and Rob's.

Gabriel had gotten stronger.

Kaitlyn could feel it through the psychic web that connected the five of them, the web that Gabriel had created. The web that would link them until one of the five died. They were all psychics: Rob was a healer and

4

Kaitlyn saw the future, Lewis was psychokinetic and Anna controlled animals—but Gabriel was a telepath. He fused minds. He'd fused *their* minds, the five of them, by accident, and now they were like the arms of a starfish: separate but part of one being.

Gabriel's power had always been strongest, but now it rocked Kaitlyn with its force. His mental voice had been amused, yes—but it had also been like a white-hot poker burning the words directly into her brain.

By contrast, Lewis's thought sounded weak and distant. *I'm scared.*

Kaitlyn glanced at him quickly and saw that he hadn't meant it to be heard. That was the problem with telepathy, with the web that connected them, held them close. It held them *too* close, sometimes, throwing their private thoughts into the public forum. Leaving them totally exposed, naked to one another. Unable to hide anything.

Realization flashed through her, and she looked back at Gabriel.

"That's it, isn't it?" she said. "Why you left. It was too much for you, being so close. It was too intimate—"

"No."

"Gabriel, we all feel the same way," Anna said, picking up on Kaitlyn's theme. "We'd all like some privacy. But we're your friends—"

Gabriel's smile was savage. "I don't need friends."

"Well, you've got them, boy," Rob said softly. He moved in another step and his hand closed on Gabriel's shoulder. With a gesture that made it look easy, he turned Gabriel around.

Kaitlyn could feel Gabriel's startled outrage in the web. Rob ignored it, speaking quietly and seriously, looking Gabriel straight in the face. His anger was gone, and so was the usual defensiveness that flared between him and Gabriel, the male rivalry, the jostling for position. Rob was struggling with his pride, his internal honesty conquering it. Forcing himself to be vulnerable with Gabriel.

"We're more than friends," he said. "We're part of each other, all of us. You made us that way. You linked us together to save our lives—and now you're telling us you've defected to the bad guys? That you're our enemy?" He shook his head. "I don't believe it."

"That's because you're an idealistic idiot," Gabriel hissed, his voice as soft as Rob's, but feral and menacing. He didn't try to move out of Rob's grip. "Believe it, country boy—because if you mess with me, you're going to be sorry."

Rob shook his head. He had a look in his eyes that Kaitlyn knew well, and his jaw was at his most stubborn. "You can't fool me, Gabriel. You act like a dumb tough guy but you're not, you're smart. One of the smartest people I've ever met. You could make something of yourself—"

"I *am*—" Gabriel began, but Rob went on, gentle and relentless.

"You act like you don't care about people, but that's not true either. You saved us all from the crystal when Joyce and Mr. Z were trying to kill us with it. You saved us again when they trapped us at the Institute. You helped Kaitlyn save us from that psychic attack in the van."

And then Rob did something that astonished Kaitlyn. He actually *shook* Gabriel. Once again, startled outrage washed through the web, but before Gabriel could say anything Rob was speaking again, fierce and insistent.

"I don't know what you're trying to prove, but it's

no good. *It's no good.* You care about us; you can't change that. Why don't you just give in and admit it, Gabriel? Why don't you stop this nonsense right now?"

Kaitlyn's breath was caught in her throat. She didn't *dare* breathe, didn't dare move. Rob was walking on a tightrope above razors and knives. He was insane—but it was working.

Gabriel's body had relaxed slightly, some of the predator-tension draining out of it. And though Kaitlyn couldn't see his eyes, she guessed that they were lightening, a warm gray instead of cold. His presence in the web was warming, too; Kaitlyn no longer got images of stalactites and glaciers. Under the burning heat of Rob's golden eyes, Gabriel's icebergs were cracking up.

"We all care about you," Rob said, never letting up the intensity. "And your place is right here. Come back to us and help us get rid of Mr. Z, okay? Okay, Gabriel?"

And then he made his mistake.

He'd been speaking vehemently, throwing his words into Gabriel's face, and Gabriel had been listening as if he couldn't help it. Almost as if he were hypnotized. But now Rob switched to nonverbal communication to punch his message directly into Gabriel's mind. Kaitlyn knew why he did it— telepathy was forceful and intimate. Too intimate. Her cry of warning was lost as Gabriel snapped.

Come back, Rob was saying. *Come back, Gabriel— okay?*

Kaitlyn felt fury building in Gabriel like a tsunami. *Rob,* she thought. *Rob, don't—*

Leave me ALONE!

The mental shout was like a physical blow. Literal-

7

ly. It threw Rob backward, body spasming in total reflex as the signals from his own brain scrambled. He fell with every muscle contracted, his face twisted, his fingers clawed. Kaitlyn felt a spasm of sheer terror on his behalf. She wanted to run to him, but she couldn't. Gabriel was between them and her legs wouldn't move. Anna and Lewis stood frozen as well.

I don't need any of you, Gabriel said, still with enough force to numb Kaitlyn's mind. *You're wrong about me. I'm no part of you. You can't even imagine what I am, what I've become.*

"I can," Kaitlyn gasped. She was thinking of what Mr. Zetes's crystal had done to him, what it had made him. A psychic vampire, who needed to drain life energy from others to live himself. She could feel the ghost of teeth in her spine, just at the base of the neck. As if a single sharp tooth were piercing the skin there.

The memory brought a certain fear, but no revulsion. And anxious as she was to get to Rob and help him, she wanted to help Gabriel, too.

"It's not your fault, Gabriel," she whispered. "You think you're evil because of what you can do with your mind, because of what the crystal made you do. But it's not your fault. You didn't ask for it. And you're not evil."

"That's where you're wrong." Gabriel had turned to face her, and she saw that he was calmer. But the ice was back in his eyes, the cold, lucid madness that was more terrifying than any rage. When he smiled, gooseflesh broke out on Kait's arms.

"I've known what I am for a long time," he said conversationally. "The crystal didn't change me, it just enhanced my abilities. And it made me accept myself." His smile widened, and Kaitlyn had a primal instinct to run. "If you've got the darkness in your nature, you might as well enjoy it. Might as well go where you belong."

"To Mr. Zetes," Anna whispered, her lovely, high-cheekboned face drawn with disgust.

Gabriel shrugged. "He has a vision. He thinks psychics like me have a place in the world—on top. I'm superior to the rest of the lousy race, I'm smarter, stronger, *better*. I deserve to *rule*. And I'm not going to let any of you stop me."

Kaitlyn shook her head, struggling with words. "Gabriel—I don't believe that. You're *not*—"

"I *am*. And if you try to keep me from getting that shard, I'm going to prove it to you."

He was looking at the desk again. Kaitlyn drew herself up a little. Rob was still lying helpless on the floor; Lewis and Anna seemed frozen. There was nobody but her to stop him.

"You can't have it," she said.

"Get out of the way."

"I said, you can't have it." To her amazement, her voice was fairly steady.

He moved closer to her, his gray eyes filling her field of vision, filling the world. *Don't make me do it, Kaitlyn. I'm not your friend anymore. I'm your hunter. Go home and stay away from Mr. Z and you won't get hurt.*

Kaitlyn looked into his handsome pale face. *If you want the shard, you'll have to take it by force.*

"Whatever you say," Gabriel murmured. His eyes were the color of a spiderweb. Kaitlyn felt the touch of his mind like a searing caress and then the world exploded in pain.

2

aitlyn!"

Dimly Kait heard Rob's shout, felt him struggling to get to his feet. Then, when he couldn't, beginning to crawl. She could barely sense him for the overwhelming pain in her head.

Anna and Lewis were closer and she could hear them shouting, too.

"Let go of her!"

"What are you doing to her?"

Gabriel brushed them away and kept on doing it. The pain increased—like fire. Kaitlyn had only one memory that would compare to it: being connected to the crystal. The big crystal, the impure one, the one Mr. Zetes used for enhancing psychic powers—and for torture.

Waves of red-streaked agony that peaked very quickly and died away just as another wave was coming. Kaitlyn's own muscle tension held her rigid, standing motionless under it. Kept her from getting away, kept her from screaming. It wasn't heroism. She didn't have the air.

Stop it, damn you! Stop it!

Rob had gotten to her, somehow. His hands were on her, and golden healing energy flooded up to combat the red-streaked anguish. His powers were protecting her.

"Leave her alone," Rob said hoarsely, and pulled Kaitlyn away from Gabriel, toward the bed.

Gabriel regarded the cleared path in front of him thoughtfully. "That was all I wanted," he murmured.

He opened the middle drawer of the mahogany desk and took out the crystal shard.

Kaitlyn was gasping for breath. Rob put her down on the bed, one arm still around her protectively. Kait could sense his trembling anger, and the shocked fury of Lewis and Anna—and she was surprised to find that she herself felt very little resentment toward Gabriel. There had been a look in his eyes just before he blasted her—as if he'd had to turn himself off to do it. To squelch his own emotions.

Now he turned to face them, and the shard flashed in the bright light of Marisol's halogen lamp. It was the size and shape of a small unicorn's horn, a foot long, multifaceted. It glittered not like crystal, but like diamond.

"It's not yours," Anna said in a low voice. She and Lewis had flanked Rob and Kaitlyn, the four of them presenting a united front to Gabriel. "The Fellowship gave it to Kait."

"The Fellowship," Gabriel sneered. "Those gutless do-gooders. If I'd lived in the old days, I'd have joined a Dark Lodge and hunted them out of existence."

Not gutless, Kaitlyn thought. Gabriel's words

11

brought the faces of the Fellowship to her mind: Timon, frail but wise; Mereniang, cool and discerning; LeShan, lynx-eyed and impatient. They were the last survivors of an ancient race, the race that had used the crystals. They didn't interfere with the affairs of humanity—but they'd made an exception for Kaitlyn's group. They'd given up their own power to give Kaitlyn a weapon against Mr. Zetes.

"And now Mr. Z is forming a Dark Lodge of his own," she said, looking at Gabriel steadily.

"You could call it that. A psychic strike team. And *I'm* going to lead it," Gabriel said negligently, stroking the crystal. That was dangerous, as Kait could have told him. One of the facets cut his finger and he frowned at the drop of blood absently. He seemed to feel no danger from the others; he didn't even bother to look at them.

"This would have been useless to you anyway," he said. "You were planning to take it to the crystal, right? Put them together and set up a resonance that would shatter both."

Kaitlyn didn't know *what* the scientific theory was. LeShan had told them that this shard would destroy Mr. Z's crystal, that was all. She watched a drop of Gabriel's blood fall onto the hardwood floor.

"But to do that, you'd have to get to the crystal," Gabriel continued. "And you can't. The old man has it under a combination lock—and PK won't help with that, will it, Lewis? Eight random numbers to guess?"

He sounded almost jolly—and he was right, Kaitlyn knew. Lewis could move objects with his mind using psychokinesis, but that wouldn't help him figure out a combination.

Lewis had flushed slightly, but he didn't answer

Gabriel's question. Instead he said, "Is Lydia still in this with you?"

"Your little sweetheart?" Gabriel grinned nastily. "Better give up on her, too. She's back under her father's thumb. She never liked you, anyway."

Pity, Kaitlyn thought. Lydia Zetes was a spy and a traitor, sent by her father to snoop on them as they traveled to Canada to find the Fellowship—but Kaitlyn felt vaguely sorry for her. Being under Mr. Z's thumb was a fate she wouldn't wish on anybody.

"It's like I told Kaitlyn," Gabriel said calmly. "You might as well all go home. You can't get at the crystal. The police wouldn't believe you—the old man has them taken care of. He's taking care of the ones Anna's parents contacted, too, by the way. And the Fellowship can't even help themselves. So there's really no point in you staying. Why don't you go home before I have to hurt you again?"

Rob had been silent so far—too angry with Gabriel to find words. Now he found them, standing up to face Gabriel directly once again. Kaitlyn didn't need the web to sense his rage—it was written in every line of his body, in the burning of his golden eyes.

"You're a traitor," he told Gabriel simply. "And if you won't join us, we'll fight you. With everything we've got."

His voice was quiet, but it shook. Not just rage, Kaitlyn thought suddenly. Rob was *hurt*—he felt personally betrayed. He hadn't believed Gabriel would hurt Kait—and Gabriel had proved him wrong. It had become a battle between them, Rob and Gabriel, the two in the group who had always fought most fiercely together, felt the most antagonism for each other, taken the positions farthest apart.

And who knew how to push each other's buttons. Rob was going on, his voice not quiet now but rushed and reckless.

"You know what I think? I think Kait was wrong— it's not the web you can't stand. It's not the intimacy. It's the *freedom*. Having to make your own choices, be responsible for yourself. That's what you can't take. You'd rather be a slave to the crystal than deal with freedom."

Gabriel lowered the shard, his eyes darkening. Kaitlyn grabbed for Rob's arm, but he seemed oblivious to her.

"I'm right, aren't I?" Rob said, with a short, strange laugh, as if delighted to have hurt Gabriel. It was so vicious and contemptuous it didn't sound like Rob. "Mr. Z tells you what to do—and you *like* that. It's what you're used to, after all those years locked up in CHAD. Hell, you probably *miss* being in jail—"

Gabriel went white and hit him.

Not mentally—Kaitlyn had the impression that he was too angry for that. He hit with his fist, catching Rob square in the mouth. Rob's head jerked back and he went down.

With the fluid, easy movements of a predator, Gabriel reached for him again. Kaitlyn found herself on her feet and between them.

"No!" She fumbled for Gabriel, meaning to restrain him or at least hinder him—and somehow found herself grabbing the crystal. It was cold and hard. She held onto it and Gabriel, still trying to get to Rob, let go.

Lewis and Anna were around Gabriel now, seizing any part of him they could reach and clinging. Kaitlyn managed to detach herself from the group and back away, clutching the crystal to her chest. Gabriel didn't seem to care; his eyes were fixed on Rob.

Who was scrambling up, wiping blood from his mouth with the back of his hand. He looked savagely triumphant at having gotten Gabriel to lose control. Kaitlyn realized he wasn't thinking anymore, just feeling. He was lost in his hurt and betrayal and anger, lashing out in a way she'd never seen before.

God, we've changed, she thought, sick with dismay. We've all changed from being in such close contact with one another. Rob used to be so pure and now he's furious . . . just like a regular human being, her mind added, unasked.

And he's *wrong*—and I've got to stop this. Before the two of them actually kill each other.

"Come on," Rob was saying. "D'you have the guts to go one on one with me? No hocus-pocus, just our fists. You man enough for that, boy?"

Gabriel pulled off his jacket, despite the efforts of Anna and Lewis to keep him still. Strapped to his forearm was a knife in some kind of spring-loaded mechanism.

Oh, *great,* Kaitlyn thought. She held on to the crystal shard more tightly. She knew she should get it to safety—but where *was* safety? Gabriel could follow anywhere she went; could take the knowledge of where it was hidden out of her mind. And besides, she couldn't leave and let Gabriel and Rob fight.

She decided to gamble.

"Here's the crystal, Gabriel," she said. "I've got it—and the only way you're going to get it is the way you did before." *But I'm hoping you won't,* she added mentally. *You said yourself that it's not going to do us any good. We can't get to Mr. Z's crystal—so what*

15

difference does it make? Why not just go back and tell him you couldn't find it?

She was trying to give him a way out. If he didn't *really* want to hurt them . . .

Gabriel hesitated. His mouth was tight; his eyes hard. But she could see uncertainty in his face. He stood very still a moment, then, abruptly, he started toward her.

Kaitlyn's mind blanked out in fear and surprise. Behind her, the door opened.

"Hey, are you guys still up——?" The sleepy voice broke off.

It was Tony, Marisol's brother, wearing cutoff shorts as pajama bottoms. He was rubbing his eyes and frowning. Clearly whatever Gabriel had done to keep the Diaz family asleep had worn off.

"Who's that?" Tony demanded, staring at Gabriel. Then he blinked and the frown disappeared.

"Hey, it's you. I remember you from last time. Come back to get the *brujo,* huh?"

He seemed happier to see Gabriel than he had been to see the rest of them, Kait thought. Maybe because Gabriel was somebody he could relate to——another tough guy. Or maybe because he thought that of all of them, Gabriel was most likely to be able to get Mr. Zetes. Tony hated Mr. Z with a passion; called him "El Diablo" or "El Gato"——both names for the devil, and longed for him to be sent *abajo*——down below to hell——where he belonged.

The five who shared the web were all frozen by the presence of a stranger, like figures in a tableau. Tony went on talking cheerfully; he didn't seem to feel the tension in the room or see the blood on Rob's chin.

"I see you got the *cuchillo*——the magic knife for Marisol. I couldn't believe it when they told me. A real old-fashioned charm, right? After all those doctors said she'd never wake up—we'll show 'em!" He grinned, his usually sullen features almost glowing. He did everything but slap Gabriel on the back.

Kaitlyn looked at Gabriel sharply, saw what she'd suspected—that he hadn't known the shard could cure Marisol. Maybe she should have told him, but she hadn't liked the idea of giving Mr. Z any further information. He'd find a way of using it against them somehow.

For now, though, it had given Gabriel pause. He seemed thrown off balance by Tony's gratitude and good humor. Embarrassed.

"Well, Gabriel certainly helped us to get the shard," Kait said—and that was true enough. If Gabriel hadn't defected, the Fellowship's crystal wouldn't have been reduced to shards in the first place. "And he would want Marisol to get well."

Rob was quietly wiping his bloody mouth again. He'd backed off when Tony came in, and Kaitlyn could feel through the web that he was calming down. Gabriel looked at him, then at Kaitlyn, and finally at Tony.

"We'll have a big party when all this is over," Tony said. "A real blowout. I've got some friends in a garage band. As soon as Marisol is better." He ran a hand through his curly mahogany hair.

Kaitlyn pressed the crystal to her chest and looked at Gabriel.

He held her gaze a minute with eyes as dark and unfathomable as storm clouds. For the first time that night she consciously noticed the scar on his forehead—a crescent-shaped mark left by his encounter with Mr. Z's crystal. Right now it seemed to stand out against the pale skin.

Then, looking suddenly tired, Gabriel shrugged. His eyelids drooped, hooding those depthless eyes.

"I've got to go," he said.

"You can stay," Tony offered immediately. "There's plenty of room."

"No, I can't. But I'll be back." He said the last to Kaitlyn and Rob, with heavy emphasis. Kait couldn't mistake his meaning. "I'll be back—soon."

He picked up his jacket and walked out the door. Kaitlyn felt her breath come out in a rush. She found she was holding the crystal so hard it hurt.

Tony yawned. "So, are you guys coming to bed? I put sleeping bags on the floor."

"Just give us a minute," Rob said. "We have to talk something over."

Tony left. Rob shut the door after him, then turned to face the others.

He isn't as calm as I thought, Kaitlyn realized. Rob's jaw was set, his skin pale under its tan.

"Now," Rob said. "What to do."

Kaitlyn shifted. "He did go away," she pointed out. "Without the crystal."

Rob angled a sharp glance at her. "Are you defending him?"

"No. But—"

"Good. Because it doesn't matter if he went away. He'll be back. You heard him."

Anna opened her mouth, then shut it and sighed. She put a hand to her forehead. Her usual serenity was in tatters, but she seemed to be regaining it, gathering it around her like a cloak. "Rob's right, Kaitlyn," she said slowly. "Gabriel did say that—and he *meant* it."

Kaitlyn lowered her arms and looked at the crystal.

It was heavy and cold, and on one facet was a pinkish smear. Gabriel's blood. "But what can we *do?*" she said.

"That's what I want to know." Lewis's round, open face was tense. "What can we do against him? He knows where we are——"

"We'll have to get out," Rob said. "That's obvious. And another thing that's obvious——Gabriel's our enemy now. I meant it when I said we'd fight him. We've got to do whatever's necessary from now on."

Kaitlyn felt very cold.

Lewis was sober. "Geez," he breathed. Then he said, "I guess if we have to stop him, we will."

"Not just that. If we have to hunt him, we will, too. We may have to destroy Mr. Zetes——and that may include Gabriel. If it does, it does. We'll do whatever it takes," Rob said. "We don't have any choice."

Lewis looked even less happy, but he nodded slowly, scratching his nose. Frightened, Kaitlyn turned to Anna.

Anna's lovely face was set. "I agree," she said quietly. "Although I hope he'll come to his senses and it won't be necessary——for now he's our enemy. We have to treat him that way." Her dark eyes were sad but stern. Kaitlyn understood——Anna's nature was peaceful, but she had the pragmatism of Nature itself. Sometimes hard choices had to be made, sometimes even sacrifices.

They were all in agreement, all united against Gabriel. And they were looking at Kaitlyn.

That was when Kaitlyn realized what she had to do.

It came to her in a dazzling burst of inspiration, almost like one of her pictures. A crazy plan, completely insane——but she had to do *something*. She couldn't let Rob destroy Gabriel—not only for Gabriel's sake, but for Rob's. If he succeeded, he would be changed forever.

The first item in her plan was not to let anyone know she was planning it.

So she composed her face and did her best to veil her thoughts. It wasn't easy to hide things from mind-mates, but she'd gotten a lot of practice in the past week or so. Looking as resigned and grim as possible, she said, "I agree, too."

She was worried that they might be suspicious— but she was with three of the most unsuspicious people in the world. Rob nodded, looking genuinely grim and resigned himself, Anna shook her head sadly, and Lewis sighed.

"We'll hope for the best," Rob said. "Meanwhile, I guess we should get some sleep. We'll have to get up early and get moving."

Which means I don't have much time, Kaitlyn thought, and then she tried to smoke-veil that, too. "It's a good idea," she said, going over to the desk and putting the crystal shard back in.

Lewis said good night and left, chewing one thumbnail and looking wistful. About Gabriel? Kaitlyn wondered. Or Lydia? Anna departed for the bathroom and Kait and Rob were left alone.

"I'm sorry about all this," Rob said. "And especially sorry he hurt you. That was—unspeakable." His eyes were dark, dark gold.

"It doesn't matter." Kaitlyn was still cold—and drawn to Rob's warmth like a moth to a flame. Especially now, when there might be no tomorrow . . . but he couldn't know that. She reached for him and he took her in his arms.

Their first kiss was a little desperate, on both sides. Then Rob calmed down, and his tranquility spread to Kait. Oh, nice. Warm tingles, warm golden haze.

It was harder now to cloak her thoughts from him. But she had to, he couldn't suspect that they were going to be separated for the first time since they'd met. Kaitlyn clung to him and concentrated on thinking about how much she loved him. How she wanted to engrave him on her memory . . .

"Kait, are you all right?" he whispered. He held her face between his hands, searching her eyes.

"Yes. I just—want to be close." She couldn't get close enough.

You've changed me, she thought. Not just showing me that boys aren't all pond scum. You've made me different, made me look at the broader picture. Given me vision.

Oh, Rob, I love you.

"I love you, Kait," he whispered back.

And *that* meant it was time to stop. She was losing her control; he was reading her thoughts. Reluctantly Kaitlyn pulled back.

"You said it yourself. We're going to need our sleep," she told him.

He hesitated, grimacing. Then nodded, yielding. "See you tomorrow."

"Sleep well, Rob."

You're so good, Rob, she thought as the door closed behind him. And so protective of me. You wouldn't let me do it. . . .

There was a map of Oakland on the desk; they'd bought it to find their way back to Marisol's house. She put it in her duffel bag with the rest of her worldly possessions—a change of clothes bought with the

Fellowship's money and her art kit—and pulled a pair of underwear over it. Maybe there was a way to leave the bag in the bathroom . . . yes, and she could wear a nightgown over her clothing. . . .

"Need something?" Anna's voice said from behind her. Guilt stricken, Kaitlyn froze in place.

3

Blank your mind! Kaitlyn told herself.

She'd been caught red-handed, thinking about things that would *make* Anna suspicious—if Anna had been listening. And everything tonight depended on Anna not suspecting.

"Just trying to figure out what to wear tomorrow," Kait said lightly, giving the bag a final rummage-through. "Not that I have much choice; I'm beginning to feel like Thoreau."

"With his one old suit?" Anna laughed, and Kaitlyn felt the knot in her stomach ease. "Well, I'm sure Marisol would lend you something if she knew what an emergency it was. Why don't you look in the closet?" Anna was going to the closet herself as she spoke. "Whew! This girl liked clothes. I bet we can both find something to fit."

I love you, Kaitlyn thought, as Anna pulled out a long slim cotton-knit dress and said, "This looks like you, Kait." I love you and Lewis almost as much as I do Rob. You're all so *decent*—and that's why he's going to beat you if you're not careful.

She forced her mind away from that and looked around the room. Marisol's room was like Marisol herself—an unpredictable mixture. Neat with messy, old with new. Like the big mahogany desk, with its silky-ruddy finish scratched and stained, as if it had been given by a loving grandmother to a careless teenager who used it for mixing perfume and storing a CD player. Or the leather miniskirt peeping out of a hamper just below the picture of the Virgin Mary.

A pair of expensive sunglasses were lying half under the bed's dust ruffle. Kait picked them up and absently twisted one gold earpiece back into shape.

"How about this?" Anna was saying, and Kait whistled. It was a very sexy, very feminine dress: spandex bodice fitting to just below the hips then flaring to a sheer chiffon skirt. Tiny gold clasps held the cap sleeves. A *radical* dress, black, that would make the wearer look slim as a statue.

"For you?" Kait said.

"No, you, dummy. It would make the boys swallow their tongues." Anna started to put the dress back. "Come to think of it, you don't need any more boy trouble. You've got two panting after you already."

"This kind of dress might get a girl *out* of trouble," Kait said hastily, taking the hanger. Spandex and chiffon wouldn't wrinkle, and she would need all the weapons she could gather if her plan went through. An outfit like this might make Gabriel sit up and take notice, and seducing Gabriel was item number one on her date book.

She folded the dress small and put it in her duffel bag. Anna chuckled, shaking her head.

Is this really me doing this? Kait wondered. Kaitlyn

Brady Fairchild, who used to think Levi's jeans were high fashion? But if she was going to be Mata Hari, she might as well do it thoroughly.

What she said was, "Anna? Do you think about boys?"

"Hmm?" Anna was peering into the closet.

"I mean, you seem so *wise* about them. You always seem to know what they'll do. But you don't seem to go after them."

Anna laughed. "Well, we've been pretty busy lately with other things."

Kaitlyn looked at her curiously. "Have you ever had one you really liked?"

There was the barest instant of hesitation before Anna answered. She was looking at another dress, fingering some sequins that were coming off. Then smiled and shrugged. "Yeah, I guess I found somebody worth caring for once."

"What happened?"

"Well—not much."

Kaitlyn, still watching curiously, realized with surprise that Anna's thoughts were veiled. It was like seeing lights behind a paper wall—she could sense color but not shape. Is that what my veiling looks like? she wondered, and barely had the wits to ask, "Why not?"

"Oh—it would never have worked out. He was together with somebody already. My best friend."

"Really?" Thoughts of veiling had led to thoughts of *what* she was veiling, and Kaitlyn was by now utterly distracted. She hardly knew what she was saying, much less what Anna was. "You should have gone for it. I'll bet you could have *taken* him. With your looks . . ."

Anna grinned ruefully and shook her head. "I

would never do that. It would be wrong." She put the sequinned dress back in the closet. "Now, bed," she said firmly.

"Um." Kaitlyn was still distracted. Thinking: I'm casual, I'm calm, I'm confident. She hurried to the bathroom and came back with her clothes still on under the billowing flannel nightgown she'd gotten at Anna's house.

She'd acquired it on the trip *up* to Canada, because they hadn't stopped by Anna's home in Puget Sound on the way back down. They'd accepted money and a 1956 Chevy Bel Air from the Fellowship and taken Route 101 all the way down the coast, driving all day for three days, avoiding Anna's parents. Avoiding *any* parents—they hadn't contacted Lewis's in San Francisco or Rob's in North Carolina or Kaitlyn's father in Ohio. They'd agreed on this early as a necessity; parents would only get worried and angry and would never, never agree to their kids doing what had to be done.

But from what Gabriel had said, Anna's parents had gone to the police anyway. They'd had proof of what Mr. Z was up to—files Rob had stolen from the Institute, detailing Mr. Z's experiments with his first group of students . . . but obviously even proof wasn't enough. Mr. Z had the police sewn up.

No one from the outside could take him down.

Kaitlyn sighed and pulled the covers more tightly over herself. She was focused on Anna, lying beside her in Marisol's bed; listening to Anna's breathing, monitoring Anna's presence in the web.

When she was certain Anna was asleep, she quietly slipped out from under the covers.

I'm going out to see Rob, she projected, not loud enough to wake the other girl, but loud enough, she hoped, to wiggle into Anna's subconscious. That way, if Anna noticed her missing in the next few hours, she might assume Kaitlyn was in the living room and not worry.

Kait tiptoed to the bathroom, where she'd managed to leave her duffel bag. She stripped off the flannel nightgown and crammed it on top of the black dress and Marisol's designer sunglasses. Then she crept down the hallway and noiselessly let herself out the back door.

There was no moon, but the stars were frosty-pale in the night sky. Oakland was too big a city for them to make much of a show, and for a moment Kaitlyn felt a pang of homesickness. Out by Piqua Road in Thoroughfare, the sky would be pitch-black, huge, and serene.

No time to think about that. Keep moving and find a phone booth, girl.

Back in Thoroughfare, she would have been terrified of walking around a strange city at night—not to mention daunted by the task of trying to get to *another* strange city, at least thirty or forty miles away. But she was a different Kaitlyn than she'd been back in Thoroughfare. She'd dealt with things then *that* Kaitlyn had never dreamed of, she'd traveled all the way to Canada without any adult to help, and she'd learned to rely on her own resources. Now she had no choice. She couldn't wait until morning—she'd never get away from the others in the daytime. She didn't have money for a cab. Still, there must be a way to get across the bay to San Carlos; she just had to find it.

With an almost frightening coolheadedness, she set out to find the way.

This wasn't a bad area of town, and she found a phone booth with an undamaged phone book. She looked up Public Transportation in the local area pages—thank heaven, it said that most of the buses ran twenty-four hours a day. She could even see the basic route she'd have to take: up to San Francisco to get across the water, then south down to San Carlos.

But now, how to *find* a bus that was running at this hour? Well, first thing was to find the bus line. Wincing a little, she tore the AC Transit map out of the phone book—a rotten thing to do, but this was an emergency. Using that and the map of Oakland she navigated her way to MacArthur Street, where the map showed the "N" bus running all night.

Once there, she heaved a sigh of relief. A twenty-four-hour gas station at the corner of MacArthur and Seventy-third. The attendant told her that the bus ran hourly, and the next one would come at 3:07. He seemed nice, a college age boy with shiny black skin and a flattop, and Kaitlyn hung around his booth until she saw the bus approaching.

The bus driver was nice, too, and let her sit behind him. He was a fat man with an endless supply of ham sandwiches wrapped in greasy paper, which he took from a bag under his seat. He offered Kait one; she accepted politely but didn't eat it, just looked out the window at the dark buildings and yellowish street-lights.

This was *really* an adventure. Going to Canada, she'd been with the others. But now she was alone and out of mind-shot—she could scream mentally and none of them would hear. As they approached the Bay Bridge, its swooping girders lit up like Christmas, Kaitlyn felt a thrill of joy in life. She clutched her duffel bag with both hands, sitting up very straight on her seat.

When they got to the terminal where she'd have to change buses, the driver scratched under his chins. "What you want now is the San Mateo line, okay? You go across the street and wait for the Seven B—it'll be along in about an hour. They keep the terminal closed because of homeless people, so you got to wait outside." He closed the bus door, shouting, "Good luck, sweetie."

Kaitlyn gulped and crossed the street.

I'm not afraid of homeless people, she told herself. I *was* a homeless person; I slept in a vacant lot, and in a van on the beach, and . . .

But when a man with a plaid jacket over his head came toward her pushing a shopping cart, she felt her heart begin to pound.

He was coming closer and closer. She couldn't see what was in the cart; it was covered with newspapers. She couldn't see his *face* either, she only thought it was a man because of the husky build.

He kept coming, slowly. Why slowly? So he could check her out? Kaitlyn's heart was going faster and faster, and her joy in life had disappeared. She'd been stupid, stupid to go wandering around at night by herself. If she'd only stayed in her nice safe bed . . .

The figure under the plaid jacket was almost on her now. And there was no place to run. She was on a deserted street in a dangerous city and she couldn't even see a phone booth. The only thing she could think of to do was sit up straight and pretend she didn't even see him. Act as if she weren't afraid.

He was right in front of her now. For an instant a streetlight shone into the hood of his jacket, and Kaitlyn saw his face.

An old man, with grizzled hair and gentle features.

He looked a little baffled and his lips moved as he walked—as he *shuffled*. That was why he was going so slowly, because he was old.

Or, Kaitlyn thought suddenly, maybe because he's weak or hungry. It would make *me* hungry to push a shopping cart around at four o'clock in the morning.

It was one of those moments when impulse overrode thought. Kaitlyn pulled the ham sandwich out of her duffel bag.

"Want a sandwich?" she said, which was exactly what the bus driver had said to her. "It's Virginia ham."

The old man took the sandwich. His eyes wandered over Kaitlyn for a moment and he gave a smile of astonishing sweetness. Then he shuffled on.

Kaitlyn felt very happy.

She was cold and tired, though, by the time the bus came. It wasn't a nice bus like the "N." It had a lot of graffiti on the outside and split vinyl seats on the inside. There was chewing gum on the floor and it smelled like a bathroom.

But Kaitlyn was too sleepy to care, too sleepy to ask to sit behind the driver. She didn't pay much attention to the tall man in the torn overcoat until he got off the bus with her.

Then she realized he was following her. It was nine or ten blocks walk to the Institute, and by the third block she was sure. What hadn't happened in the depths of Oakland or the wilds of San Francisco was happening here.

Or . . . he might be okay. Like the man with the shopping cart. But the man of the cart hadn't been following her.

What to do? Knock on somebody's door? This was a residential neighborhood, but all the houses were dark. Run? Kaitlyn was a good runner; she could probably outdistance the man if he wasn't in good shape.

But she couldn't seem to make herself do *anything.* Her legs just kept walking mechanically down Exmoor Street, while shivers ran up her spine at the thought of him behind her. It was as if she were caught in some dream, where the monsters couldn't get her as long as she didn't show she was afraid.

When she turned a corner she glanced back at him. Foxy red hair—she could see that under a streetlight. His clothes were ragged but he looked strong, athletic. Like somebody who could easily overtake a seventeen-year-old girl running.

That was what she saw with her eyes. With her other sense—the one that sometimes showed her the future —she got no picture but a distinct impression. *Bad.* This man was *bad,* dangerous, full of evil thoughts. He wanted to do something bad to *her.*

Everything seemed to go clear and cold. Time stretched and all Kait's instincts were turned to survival. Her brain was whirring furiously, but no matter which way she turned the situation looked the same. Very bad. No inspiration came about to save herself.

And underneath her thoughts ran a sickening litany: I should have known I couldn't get away with this. Wandering around at night on my own . . . I should have *known.*

Think of something, girl. *Think.* If you can't run, you'd better find shelter, fast.

All the houses around her looked asleep, locked-up. She had a horrible certainty that no one would let her in . . . but she had to do *something.* Kait felt a sort of wrenching in her guts—and then she had turned and was heading for the nearest house, taking the single porch step in a jump and landing on the welcome mat. Something inside her cringed from banging on the door, even in this extremity, but she clamped down on the cringe and *did* it. Hollow bangs echoed—not loud enough, to Kait's ears. She saw a doorbell, pushed on it frantically. She kept pounding, using the side of her fist because it hurt less than using her knuckles.

Inside, she could hear only silence. No reaction to her noisy intrusion. No footsteps running to the door.

Oh, God, *answer!* Come here and answer your door, you idiots!

Kaitlyn looked behind her and her heart nearly jumped out of her body.

Because the foxy man was *there;* he was standing on the walkway of the house. Looking at her.

And he was veryveryvery bad. His mind was full of things that Kaitlyn couldn't sense directly, but that when put together sounded like one long scream. He'd done things to other girls—he wanted to do them to her.

No sound from the house. No help. And she was cornered prey here on the porch. Kait made her decision in an instant. She was off the porch and running, running for the Institute, before the man could move a step.

She heard her own pounding footsteps in the street —and pounding feet behind her. Her breath began to sob.

And it was dark and she was *confused.* She didn't know which way the Institute was anymore. Somewhere around here she turned left—but *where?* It was a street that sounded like a flower or plant—but she couldn't read street signs anyway.

That street looked familiar. Kait swerved toward it, trying to get a glimpse of the sign. Ivy Street—was that right? There was no time to debate. She veered down the street, trying to push her legs into going faster . . . and realized almost instantly that it was a mistake.

A cul-de-sac. When she reached the end, she'd be caught.

She glanced behind her. He was there, running, overcoat flapping like the wings of a bird of prey. He was ungainly but very fast.

She wasn't even going to make it to the end of the cul-de-sac.

If she ran to a house, he'd grab her as she stood on the porch. If she slowed, he'd tackle her from behind. If she tried to double back, he'd cut her off.

The only thing she could think of to do was stand and fight.

Once again, the feeling of clear coldness swept over her. Right, then. She pulled up short, staggering a little, and whirled. She was standing in the widest part of the cul-de-sac, surrounded by parked cars.

He saw her and stumbled, slowing down, hesitating. Then, at a shambling half-run, he started toward her again. Kaitlyn stood her ground.

She was glad she hadn't dropped her duffel bag. Maybe she could use it as a weapon. Or maybe there was something *in* it to use. . . .

No, everything was too soft. Except the pencils, but they were in her art kit. She'd never get them out in time.

Then I'll use my fingers to stab his eyes out, she thought savagely. And my knees and my feet and fists. Adrenaline was singing in her veins; she was almost *glad* of the chance to fight. The things she sensed inside him made her want to rip him to pieces. He'd killed, he was a killer.

"Come on, you creep," she said, and realized she was saying it out loud.

He came. He was grinning, a crazy-happy grin. His eyes were crazy, too. Kaitlyn tensed her muscles and then he was on her.

4

Gabriel was blocking the world out, but the scream came through.

He was pacing in front of the Institute, loitering. He'd been out all night, and didn't particularly want to go in. Not that anyone inside now would bother him—but he still had an impulse to avoid the place. He'd screwed up; he hadn't gotten the crystal shard. And tonight he'd have to explain to *him*.

Zetes. Gabriel felt a muscle in his jaw twitch. He understood now why Marisol had been so afraid of the old man. He had a sort of malevolent power about him, a power that was best observed in day-to-day living. He seemed to drain the will out of everyone around him. Not suddenly, the way Gabriel drained life energy, but slowly. People around him began to feel nervous and exhausted—and dazed. Like birds looking into the eyes of a snake.

A quiet form of terrorization.

Gabriel didn't intend to be terrorized. But now that

he'd chosen his path, he needed Zetes. The old man had the structure, the organization, the contacts. Gabriel planned to use all those things on his journey to the top.

He was debating going in when the scream sliced through his consciousness. It wasn't a vocal sound, purely mental. It was composed of hate and anger as well as fear. And it was Kaitlyn.

Close. North and west of him, he thought. He was moving before he thought anything else.

And he probably couldn't have explained why if anyone had asked him.

He moved with the smooth long steps of a hunting wolf. The scream came again—the sound of someone fighting for her life. Gabriel moved faster, homing in on it.

Ivy Street. It was coming from down there—and now he could see it, in the streetlights at the end of the cul-de-sac. He couldn't hear anything except mentally; Kaitlyn never did scream out loud when she was in trouble.

Gabriel reached the grappling figures at a dead run. A red-haired man was on top of Kaitlyn, and she was biting, kicking, and clawing. The man was considerably damaged but sure to win in the end. He was heavier and stronger; he could outlast her.

Déjà vu, Gabriel thought. Once in back of the Institute he'd found another man attacking Kaitlyn—a man who'd turned out to be from the Fellowship. This one, Gabriel thought, eyeing the unwashed hair and unsavory appearance of Kaitlyn's attacker, was unlikely to be anything but a bum.

He could just leave things as they were. The old man would be happy to hear Kaitlyn was dead, and it would mean one less person keeping the shard from them. But . . .

All these thoughts flashed through Gabriel's mind in seconds. Before he'd even consciously come to a conclusion, he was reaching for the man.

He tangled a hand in the back of the dirty overcoat and pulled, yanking the man up. Kaitlyn rolled out from under, and he could hear the surprise in her mind. *Gabriel!*

So she hadn't seen him. Well, she'd been busy trying to stay alive. The man in the overcoat was reacting now, pulling away. He saw Gabriel and threw a punch.

Gabriel ducked around it. He jerked his arm and the knife in his sleeve *snicked* out. His hand closed around it, feeling the welcome weight, the smoothness of the handle.

The man's eyes got big.

Just like Wolverine, Gabriel thought, cutting the knife in front of him in a practice move. The red-haired man's eyes followed it. He was scared; Gabriel could already taste the flavor of his fear.

But don't worry about the knife, he thought, knowing the man couldn't hear him. That's just a distraction, to keep you watching . . . while I do *this*. . . .

Gabriel's other hand rose almost gracefully, gracefully and stealthily, and touched the man on the back of the spine. Just above the soiled collar of the overcoat, just at the nape of the neck.

His fingers made contact with skin, found the transfer point. He could find it easier with his mouth, but he wasn't going any nearer this filthy derelict than he had to. There was a feeling of breakage, as if something was tearing loose. The red-haired man stiffened violently, his muscles jerking. Then Gabriel felt it—the rush of energy, like blue-white light streaking up from the transfer point, fountaining into the air. Into Gabriel's fingers, filling channels and rushing through them, warming his entire body.

Ahhhhh.

It was something like a cold drink on a hot day—a cold drink in a tall glass, with ice cubes clinking against the inside and drops of water condensing on the outside. And it was something like getting your second wind when running—a sudden feeling of strength and peace and vigor. And it was something like standing on the bow of a catamaran with the wind in your face. It wasn't *much* like any of those things, but they were as close as Gabriel could get to the feelings of refreshment and vitality and excitement.

Drinking pure life, that was what it was. And even from a filthy derelict, it tasted pretty good. This guy had been more alive, in his creepy, slimy way, than most. Gabriel let go of him, then pushed the knife back into its casing.

The red-haired man gave a shudder and collapsed, falling as if he'd been deboned. On the ground, he twitched once and was still. He smelled bad.

Kaitlyn, breathing hard, was getting to her feet.

"Is he dead?" she asked.

"No, he's got a gasp or two left. But he's not at all well."

"You enjoyed that." Her eyebrows were arched in scorn and her smoky blue eyes flashed. Wispy red curls clung to her forehead; the rest of her hair was loose in a glorious flame-colored waterfall. She looked flushed and windblown and very beautiful.

Gabriel looked away angrily. He *wouldn't* think about her, he wouldn't see how beautiful she was, how fair her skin was or the way her breathing moved her chest. She belonged to someone else, and she meant *nothing* to him.

He said, looking at the huddled figure on the ground, "You were doing a pretty good job on him yourself."

Kaitlyn shivered, then controlled it. Her voice was softer when she answered. "I could see he was full of nasty things. His mind was . . ." She shivered again.

"You could see into his mind?" Gabriel asked sharply.

"Not exactly. I could *sense* it somehow—sort of like a feeling or a smell. I couldn't tell exactly what he was thinking." She looked up at Gabriel, hesitated, then took a deep breath. "I'm sorry. I didn't say thank you. But I *am* glad you showed up. If you hadn't . . ." Her voice trailed off again.

He ignored this last. "Maybe being in the web has made you slightly telepathic for other people—or maybe that guy was slightly telepathic." He touched the overcoat with the toe of his running shoe. Then he looked at Kait. "Where are the others?"

Kaitlyn drew herself up, looked back calmly. "What others?"

"You know what others." Gabriel stretched out his senses, listening for the slightest hint of their presence. Nothing. He narrowed his eyes at Kaitlyn. "They've got to be around somewhere. You wouldn't come out here alone."

"Wouldn't I? I *am* alone. I came on the bus; it was easy. Aren't you going to ask why?"

Behind her, the sky was green and palest pink, shading to ultramarine in the west. The last stars were going out, the first light was touching her hair with red-gold. She stood slim and proud as some medieval witch princess against the dawn. Gabriel had to work to keep his face expressionless, to keep his presence in the web icy.

"All right," he said. "What are you doing here?"

"What do you mean, she's *gone?*" Rob demanded.

"She's gone," Anna repeated miserably. "I woke up and looked and there she wasn't. She isn't *here.*"

Lewis rolled over in his sleeping bag, squinting and scratching. "Did you check in the, uh . . ."

"Of course I've checked in the bathroom. I've looked *everywhere,* and she's just not anywhere. Her bag is gone, too, Rob."

"What?" It came out a yell. Anna clapped a hand over his mouth, and Rob stared at her over it.

If her bag's gone, she's gone, he said telepathically after a moment.

That's what I've been telling you, Anna replied. Her beautiful dark eyes were wide but calm. Anna always could keep her head in a crisis—and Rob was close to losing his. Ever since last night his emotions had been in a turmoil.

With an effort he collected himself. *No, I mean that she's gone for a while—and probably of her own free will. Somebody kidnapping her wouldn't have taken the bag.*

"But—why would she leave?" Lewis asked, sitting up. "I mean, she *wouldn't* leave, but if she did leave—well, why?"

Rob looked past the dark, heavy shapes of the living room furniture to the window. It was just dawn.

"I think . . . she's maybe gone to the Institute."

The other two stared at him.

"No," Anna said.

Rob lifted his shoulders, lip caught between his

lower teeth. He was still looking out the window. "I think yes."

"But *why?*" Lewis said. Rob barely heard him. He was looking at the sky, translucently blue, like glass. Kait was out there somewhere. . . .

"Rob!" Lewis was shaking him. *"Why* would she have gone to the Institute?" he demanded.

"I don't know," Rob said, coming back to earth. "But she might have an idea she can influence Gabriel —or maybe she wants to try something on Mr. Zetes."

Anna and Lewis audibly let air out of their lungs. "I thought—I mean I thought you were saying . . ."

Rob blinked at him, bewildered.

"He thought you were saying that Kait defected like Gabriel," Anna said crisply. *"I* knew she didn't, but I thought maybe *you* thought she did."

"Of course she wouldn't do that," Rob said, shocked. It was hard for him to understand other people sometimes—they seemed so quick to think the worst about each other, even their friends. He knew better; Kaitlyn wasn't capable of anything evil.

"But she must have gone in the middle of the night," Lewis was saying. "You think she took the car?"

"The car's out front. I looked before I woke you up," Anna said. "I don't know *how* she could make it."

"She'd find a way," Rob said briefly. Kaitlyn was silk and fire—over a steel-hard core of determination. "No, she'll get there, if that's where she's going. The question is, what do we do about it?"

"What *can* we do?" Lewis said.

There were sounds of stirring in the back of the

house. Marisol's parents. Rob glanced that way, then back out the window.

"We'll have to get to her somehow. Find her and get her out of there."

"Get her out," Anna said quietly. It wasn't a question, it was a confirmation.

"We *have* to," Rob said. "I don't know what she has in mind, but it's not going to work. Not in that house of lunatics. They're dangerous. They'll kill her."

"I came to see you," Kaitlyn said, and moved closer to him.

She could tell he wasn't buying it.

"It's *true*. Look at me, feel my thoughts. I came here to see you, Gabriel."

She was taking a chance. But she *had* come to see him, that much was true, and after he'd just saved her life she was genuinely glad to see him. He could sense that much safely. And she was betting he wouldn't search below the surface, because that would mean getting close, letting *her* sense *him*. She had the strong feeling he didn't want that.

He was looking at her hard, his gray eyes narrowed against the light. Beautiful north light, slanting around them, making the modest houses look enchanted, making even Gabriel look golden and warm. She could only guess how it made her look.

Gabriel dropped his eyes. His psychic senses had brushed her mind as lightly as a moth's wing. "So you came to see me," he said.

"I've missed you," Kaitlyn said, and that was also true. She'd missed his razor wit and the mocking humor that glinted behind his eyes and his strength in the web. "I want to join you."

It was such a whopping huge lie that she expected to

feel the alarms going off in his head. But he'd withdrawn his mental probing and veiled himself. He wouldn't even look at her properly.

"Don't be stupid," Gabriel said, in a voice suddenly gone weak.

Kaitlyn saw her advantage and pounced. "I *did*. I decided last night. I don't like Mr. Z, but I think some of the things he says are true. We have infinite possibilities—we just need room. Freedom. And we *are* superior to other people."

Gabriel seemed to have gathered himself. "You don't go in for that stuff."

"Why shouldn't I? I'm tired of running. I want to be with you, and I want power. What's wrong with that?"

His mouth had gone hard. "Nothing's wrong—only you don't believe it."

"Test me." Kaitlyn's heart was pounding with the risk. "Gabriel, I didn't know what we had together until you left. I care about you." This was it, the time to see whether she was true Hollywood material. She stepped even closer to Gabriel, almost touching him. "Believe me."

If he wanted, he could reach into her mind and rip the truth out. Her thin shields wouldn't hold against him.

But he didn't try to probe her brain. He kissed her instead.

Kaitlyn surrendered to the kiss deliberately—she knew she had to, and she felt a flash of triumph. Small-town girl makes good. A star is born!

Then the triumph was swept away by something much stronger and deeper. Something fierce and joyous—and *pure*. They were clinging together, he was holding her as hard as she was holding him.

Electricity seemed to arc between them. Everywhere they touched Kaitlyn could feel the sparks. His hand tangled in her hair, and she was frighteningly moved by the tiny tugs, the little pain it caused as his fingers worked. His lips brushed against hers again and again.

An ache was starting inside Kaitlyn. They were together, *together,* so close, and she wanted to be closer. A trembling thrill raced through her—and then a flash of light. His fingers were on the nape of her neck.

A flash of light—it was beginning. The sparks becoming a blue-white torrent. In a moment the transfer point would open, and her energy would flood into him.

The ultimate sharing—but she *couldn't.* Their minds would be open to each other. She would have no shields—he would see everything.

Kaitlyn tried to pull away . . . but it didn't work. He was holding her and she couldn't seem to let go of him. She didn't have the will—and in a moment he would *see*—

A garage door roared to life.

Kaitlyn jumped and was saved. Gabriel lifted his head, looking at a house near them. Kaitlyn took the moment to step away.

The world was coming to life around them. It wasn't dawn but daylight. The door to another house was opening; a cat was running up a walkway. No one had noticed the tall boy standing in the street kissing a girl, or the crumpled figure at their feet.

"But they'll see us in a minute," Kaitlyn whispered. "Let's go."

They walked quickly. At the intersection, Kaitlyn looked at him. "Which way to the Institute?"

"You really want to go there?" He looked doubtful,

but not contemptuous as before. She'd convinced him.

"I want to be with you."

Gabriel was confused. Confused and vulnerable—there was something fragile in his eyes. "But—I hurt you."

"You didn't want to." Kaitlyn was sure of that suddenly. She'd thought so before, but now she was *sure*.

"I don't know," he said shortly. "I don't know anything anymore."

"*I* know. Forget about it." She could tell he was still bewildered, but she figured that was probably good. The more off balance, the less he'd be likely to analyze her. She was still dizzy and bewildered herself from that kiss.

Oh, God, what am I getting myself into?

She decided to think about it later.

"Is Joyce still running things?" Joyce Piper was the woman who'd recruited them both last winter—who'd made the Institute seem like a legitimate place. Even now Kaitlyn had a hard time believing she was as bad as Mr. Z.

"If you can call it running things. She's supposed to be in charge, but—well, you'll see."

Kaitlyn felt a surge of victory, suppressed it. He wasn't arguing anymore. He was assuming she'd come, and that they'd let her in.

I'm going to do it, she thought. She suddenly realized that it was wonderful good luck that she was arriving with Gabriel. He was going to help her immeasurably.

As they neared the Institute she thought, stand tall, walk tall. She held her head up. The first time she'd come here she'd been overwhelmed by anxiety. Worry about her new roommates—would they like her, would they accept her? Now she had much more serious things to worry about, but she had a purpose. She knew she looked cool and confident, almost regal.

She reached into her duffel bag and pulled out Marisol's sunglasses. Put them on, flicked back her hair.

Now I'm ready.

Gabriel glanced at her. "Those new?"

"Well, I don't figure Marisol needs them anymore." She saw him raise his eyebrows at her new hardheartedness.

The Institute was *purple*. Well, of course she remembered that, but it was still a shock to see how truly purple it was. A wild thrill of homesickness ran through her.

"Come on," Gabriel said, and led her to the door. It was locked. He rattled in exasperation.

"I forgot the key—"

"What about your new talent for breaking and entering?"

But the door opened. Joyce was standing there, her short blond hair slick and wet. She was wearing a pink sweater and leggings.

As always, an aura of energy surrounded her, as if she might suddenly spring into action at any moment. Her aquamarine eyes were sparkling with life.

"Gabriel, where have—" She broke off, her eyes widening. She'd seen Kaitlyn.

For a moment they just stood and looked at each other. Under her cool exterior, Kaitlyn's heart was pounding. She *had* to convince Joyce, she had to. But she could feel the waves of suspicion radiating from the blond woman.

Once, Joyce had fooled her, had fooled all of them.

Now it was Kaitlyn's turn. Kait felt just like one of those Federal agents infiltrating the Mafia.

And you know what they do to *them,* she thought.

"Joyce—" she began, making her voice gentle and persuasive.

Joyce didn't even glance at her. "Gabriel," she said in a grating whisper, "get her the hell out of here."

5

Kaitlyn stared at Joyce in dismay. There was a buzzing in her ears, and she couldn't speak.

Gabriel saved her. "Wait until you hear what she has to say."

Joyce glanced from one of them to the other. Finally she said, "Did you get the crystal shard?"

"I couldn't find it," Gabriel answered without any discernible pause. "They have it hidden someplace else. But what difference does it make?"

"What *dif*—" Joyce clamped her lips together and threw a glance behind her, as if worried she'd be overheard. "The difference is that *he's* going to be here tonight, wanting it."

"Look, are you going to let us in or not?"

Joyce let out a stifled breath, turned her gem-hard eyes on Kaitlyn again. She gazed for a long moment, then she abruptly reached out and snatched the sunglasses from Kaitlyn's face. Kait was startled but wouldn't show it; she returned the aquamarine gaze steadily.

"All right," Joyce said at last. "Come in. But this had better be good."

"It's good if you want another clairvoyant," Gabriel said once they were in the living room. "You know Frost isn't very good."

Joyce sat down, one trim pink leg crossed over the other. "You've got to be kidding," she said shortly.

"I want to join you," Kaitlyn said. The buzzing was gone from her ears; she could speak in cool, nonchalant tones.

"I'm sure!" Joyce said. *Her* tone was sarcastic.

"Would I bring her here if it wasn't true?" Gabriel asked. He flashed one of his brilliant, unsettling smiles. Before Joyce could reply he added, "I've looked into her mind. She's sincere. So why don't we just cut the bull? I'm hungry."

"Why would she want to join us?" Joyce demanded. She looked shaken by Gabriel's conviction.

Kaitlyn went through her speech about believing Mr. Z's theories about psychics and supreme power. She was getting good at it by now. And, she was finding, it was fairly easy to sell it to people who wanted power themselves. It was a motivation they could understand.

At the end of the oration Joyce bit her lip. "I don't know. What about the others? Your friends."

"What about them?" Kaitlyn said coldly.

"You were involved with Rob Kessler. Don't deny it."

Kaitlyn could feel Gabriel waiting for the answer, too. "We broke up," she said. She wished, suddenly, that she had thought more about this part of the story. "I was interested in Gabriel and that made him furious. Besides," she added with happy inspiration, "he likes Anna."

She had no idea what made her say it, but it had an unexpected effect on both Joyce and Gabriel. Joyce's eyebrows went up, but some of the tightness went out of her mouth. Gabriel hissed in a sharp breath—like someone about to say, I knew it all the time.

Kaitlyn was startled. She hadn't *meant* that. Rob had never given any sign—and neither had Anna—or at least she didn't *think* so. . . .

And she couldn't think about it now. She had to stay firmly in the moment. She fixed her eyes on Joyce, who was looking torn.

"Look," Kait said. "This is straight up. I wouldn't come here if I wasn't serious—I wouldn't put my *dad* in that much danger." She held Joyce's gaze. "Because you guys can do things to him, right? I wouldn't risk that." In fact, it wasn't something she had realized until a little while ago. Mr. Z's psychics could attack over any distance, and if they found out the truth about Kait, he'd be an obvious target. Now it was too late to turn back—the only way to protect her dad was to make her act good.

"Hmm. But you went all the way to Canada to *fight* us."

"Sure. I went to the Fellowship and found it was a crock. They can't even help themselves, much less anyone else. And—it's not that I don't care about Rob and the others anymore, but I can't stick with them when they're going to lose. I want to be on the winning side."

"You and Lydia," Joyce said, grimly amused. It was another hit; Kait could tell. "Well, if nothing else I suppose we can use you as a hostage," Joyce murmured.

"In that case, can we get some breakfast?" Gabriel

asked, not waiting to see what Kaitlyn's reaction would be.

"Right," Joyce said briefly, handing Kaitlyn the sunglasses. "Nobody else is up yet. Get it yourselves."

A little different from the cheerful-homemaker attitude you had before, Kaitlyn thought, not bothering to shield it from Gabriel. He grinned.

The kitchen was different. Dirty, for one thing; there were dishes in the sink and Coke cans spilling out of the wastebasket. A cardboard box full of sloppily shut take-out containers was on the counter.

Chinese food, Kaitlyn saw. Joyce never let *us* have take-out Chinese. And those boxes of Frosted Flakes and Captain Crunch in the pantry—what had happened to Joyce's health food kick? An act?

"I told you she wasn't exactly running things anymore," Gabriel said under his breath, slanting a quirky glance at her.

Oh. Kaitlyn shrugged and poured herself a bowl of Captain Crunch.

When they were finished eating, Joyce said, "Right, go upstairs and get yourself cleaned up. You can go in Lydia's room for now—then we'll see about further arrangements when *he* comes tonight."

Kaitlyn was surprised. "Lydia's living here?"

"I told you," Gabriel said. "Under her father's thumb."

As she and Gabriel reached the landing, Kait said, "Which room do you have now?"

"The same as before." He indicated the best room in the house, the big one that had cable hookup and a balcony. Then he gave her an evil glance. "Want to share it with me? You can use the Jacuzzi. And the king-size bed."

"I think Joyce would put her foot down about *that,*" Kaitlyn said.

She didn't know which room was Lydia's, but she knocked lightly on the door of the room she used to share with Anna. Then she looked in.

Lydia, small in an oversize T-shirt, was just getting out of bed. She saw Kaitlyn and squeaked. Her eyes darted around the room, looking for an exit, then she took a sideways step toward the bathroom door.

Kaitlyn chuckled. In a way, it was a relief to see someone more scared than she was. "What's the hurry?" she said, feeling lazy and dangerous. Like Gabriel.

Lydia seemed to be paralyzed. She wriggled a little, like a worm on a hook, then she blurted, "He made me do it. I didn't want to leave you in Canada."

"Oh, Lydia, you're such a liar. You did it for the same reason I did. You wanted to be on the winning side."

Lydia's cat-tilted green eyes opened even wider. She was a pretty little thing, with a pale and delicate face and a heavy shock of black hair. Or she would have been pretty if she hadn't always looked so guilty and slinking, Kait thought.

"The same reason you did?" Lydia breathed. "You mean—Father brought you here—?"

"I came on my own, to join you guys," Kaitlyn said firmly. "Joyce said I could share this room." She swung her duffel bag over the twin bed that wasn't rumpled, and dropped it with a thump.

She'd expected Lydia to look awed or understanding. Instead, Lydia looked as if she thought Kait was crazy.

"You *came on your own* . . ." Then she stopped and shook her head. "Well, you're right about one thing,"

she said. "My father is going to win. He always wins."
She looked away, lip curling.

Kaitlyn eyed her thoughtfully. "Lydia, how come
you're at the Institute? You're not psychic—are you?"

Lydia shrugged vaguely. "My father wanted me
here. So Joyce could watch me, I think."

And you didn't really answer the question, Kaitlyn
thought. Gabriel had said that if Kait had picked up
the red-haired man's thoughts, either she or the
red-haired man must be slightly telepathic. But
Kaitlyn had been able to tell how Joyce felt about her,
and now she was getting strong feelings from Lydia. It
wasn't that she could tell exactly what they were
thinking; more that she could get a sense of their
general mood.

So I'm a telepath? It was a weird and unsettling
thought. Telepathy in the web didn't count; Gabriel
had hooked them together. But to sense other people's
feelings was something new.

Like just now she could tell that Lydia had a lot on
her mind—which meant she might be induced to talk.

"So what's it like around here?" Kaitlyn asked
casually.

Lydia's lip curled farther, but she just shrugged
again and said, "Have you met the others?"

"No. Well, I mean, I've seen their astral forms
before, on the way to Canada."

"You'll probably like those better than their real
forms."

"Well, why don't you introduce me?" Kait sug-
gested. She wasn't really as interested in the dark
psychics as in the routine around here—something
that might give her an idea where Mr. Z kept the
crystal. But any information would be helpful, and
she figured it was better to be aggressive in meeting

Mr. Z's new students. She didn't want them to think she was afraid of them.

"You *want* to see them?" Lydia was afraid of them.

"Yeah, come on, show me the psychic psychos." Kaitlyn kept her tone light and was rewarded with a faint, admiring grin. "Let's tour the zoo."

In the hallway, they nearly ran into Joyce. She glanced at them and then knocked briskly at the door of what had once been the common room for Kait's group. Without waiting for an answer, she threw the door open.

"Everybody up! Renny, you have to get to school; Mac, we start testing in ten minutes. If you want any breakfast, you'd better move it."

She moved on, to yell at another door. "Bri! School! Frost! Testing!"

Kaitlyn, with a clear view of the first room, had to keep herself from gasping.

Oh, my God, I don't believe it.

The room was now a bedroom—sort of. Like a bedroom from a flophouse, Kaitlyn thought. No, *worse*. Like a bedroom from one of those abandoned buildings you see on the news. Across one wall the words "NO FEAR" were spray-painted. *Spray-painted*. Most of the curtains were down and one of the windows in the alcove was broken. There was a large hole in the plaster of one wall and another in the door.

And the room was filthy. It wasn't just the motorcycle helmet and the traffic cones on the floor, or the stray bits of clothing draped over every piece of furniture, or the cups overflowing with cigarette butts. There were cookie crumbs and ashes and potato chips mashed into the carpet, and mud on almost everything. Kaitlyn marveled at how they'd managed to get it so dirty in such a short time.

A boy wearing only boxer shorts was standing up. He was big and lanky, with hair so short it was almost nonexistent, and dark, evil, knowing eyes. A skinhead? Kaitlyn wondered. He looked like the kind of guy you would hire as an assassin, and his mind felt like the red-haired man's.

"Jackal Mac," Lydia whispered. "His real name's John MacCorkendale."

Jackal eyes, Kaitlyn thought. That's it.

The other boy was younger, Kaitlyn's age. He had skin the color of creamed coffee and a little, lean, quick body. His face was narrow, his features clean and sharp. The glasses perched on his nose did nothing to make him look less tough. A smart kid gone bad, Kait thought. The brains of the operation? She couldn't get a clear feeling about his mood.

"That's Paul Renfrew, Renny," Lydia whispered— and ducked. Jackal Mac had thrown a size twelve combat boot at her.

Kaitlyn ducked, too. Then she stood frozen as the huge guy rushed toward them, all arms and legs.

"What are you doing here? What do you want?" he snarled, right in Kaitlyn's face.

Oh, Lord, she thought. His *tongue* is pierced. It was, with what looked like a metal bolt.

Renny had come, too, light as a sparrow, his eyes merry and malicious. He circled Kaitlyn, picked up a strand of her hair by the ends.

"Ouch! That burns!" he said. "But the curves are okay." He smoothed a hand over Kait's behind. "I like her better in the flesh."

Kaitlyn reacted without thinking. She whirled

around and her hand made sharp contact with Renny's cheek. It knocked his glasses askew.

"You don't ever do that," she said through her teeth. It brought back every moment of loathing she'd ever felt for a boy. Boys, with their big meaty hands and their big sloppy grins . . . she pulled her arm back in preparation for another slap.

Jackal Mac caught her wrist from behind. "Hey, she fights! I like that."

Kaitlyn jerked her hand out of his grasp. "You haven't seen anything yet," she told them, and gave her best wolfish grin. It wasn't acting. This was genuine, from the heart.

They both laughed, although Renny was rubbing his cheek.

Kaitlyn turned on her heel. "Come on, Lydia. Let's meet the others."

Lydia had been crouching by the stairway. Now she straightened up slightly and hurried toward the second door Joyce had shouted at. It was the room Rob and Lewis had shared in the old days.

The door was ajar; Lydia pushed it open. Kaitlyn braced herself for more destruction.

She wasn't disappointed. Once again the curtains were down, although here they'd been replaced by black sheets. There was a black candle burning on the dresser, dripping wax, and an upside-down pentagram scrawled on the mirror in lipstick. *Glamour* magazines lay open on the floor, and there was the inevitable scattering of clothing and garbage.

There was a girl on each of the twin beds.

"Laurie Frost," Lydia said. She didn't seem quite so afraid of the girls. "Frost, this is Kaitlyn—"

"I know her," the girl said sharply, sitting up. She had blond hair even lighter than Joyce's, and much messier. Her face was beautiful, although the permanently flared nostrils gave it a look of perpetual disdain. She was wearing a red lace teddy and as she raised a hand to flick hair out of her eyes Kaitlyn saw that she had long silvery nails. They were pierced with tiny rings like earrings.

"She's one of *them*. The ones who ran away," Frost said in a menacing hiss.

"Hey, yeah," the other girl said.

There was no need for Lydia to introduce her. Kaitlyn recognized her from a picture on a file folder in Mr. Z's office. Except that the picture had been of a pretty, wholesome girl with dark hair and a vivid face. Now she was still pretty—in a bizarre way. There were streaks of cerulean blue in her hair, and black smudges of makeup surrounding her eyes. Her face was hard, her jaw belligerent.

Sabrina Jessica Gallo, Kaitlyn thought. We meet at last.

"I know you, too," Kaitlyn said. She kept her voice cool and returned Bri's stare boldly. "And I'm not running away now. I came back."

Bri and Frost looked at each other, then back at Kait. They burst into nasty laughter, Bri barking, Frost tittering.

"Right back into the mousetrap," Frost said, flicking her long, silvery nails. "It's Kaitlyn, right? What do they call you, Kaitlyn? Kaitykins? Kitty? Kit Cat?"

Bri took it up. "Kit Kat? Pretty Kitty? Pretty Pretty?"

They dissolved into laughter again.

"We'll have to make the Kitty Kat welcome," Frost said. Her wide, pale blue eyes were spiteful but slightly unfocused. Kaitlyn wondered if she were hung over from something—or maybe that was just the way these people *were*. The Fellowship had sensed insanity in them, and what Kaitlyn sensed now was that each of them was a little bit *off*. Aggressive, malicious—but not very focused. As if there were an inner fogginess in each of them. They weren't even properly suspicious; they weren't asking the right questions.

And Kait wasn't sure what to do with them while they were pointing and giggling at her like kindergartners.

"Sabrina and Frost, I said *now!*" Joyce's voice came from the corridor, cracking like a whip. The girls kept giggling. Joyce pushed past Kaitlyn like a blond meteor and began yelling at them, picking clothes up off the floor.

Kaitlyn shook her head, putting on an expression of genteel astonishment for Joyce's benefit. Then she turned to Lydia.

"I think I've seen enough," she said, and made an exit.

A few minutes later Joyce came into Lydia's room. Her sleek hair was ruffled and she was flushed, but her aquamarine eyes were still hard.

"You can stay in this room today," she said to Kaitlyn. "I don't want you going downstairs while I'm doing testing."

"That's fine with me. I didn't get any sleep last night."

"Good luck napping," Joyce said grimly.

But in a surprisingly short time, the upper floor was still. Lydia, Renny, and Bri had departed for school; Jackal Mac and Frost were presumably being tested. Gabriel's door was locked.

Kaitlyn lay down on her old familiar bed—and realized how tired she really was. She felt wrung out, drained not only of energy, but of emotion. She'd meant to lie awake and make a plan, but she fell asleep almost instantly.

She woke a long time later. Warm, diffuse afternoon light filled the room. Silence filled her ears.

She got up and grabbed for the headboard as a wave of giddiness swept her. Breathing slowly, she held her head down until she felt steadier.

Then she crept in stocking feet to the door.

Still silence. She went to the stairway and turned her head, ear pointed downstairs. No sound. She descended quietly.

If Joyce saw her, she'd say she was hungry, and when was dinnertime anyway?

But Joyce didn't appear. The lower floor seemed deserted. Kaitlyn was alone in the house.

Okay, don't panic. This is terrific, the perfect opportunity. What do you want to look at first?

If I were a big ugly crystal, where would I be?

One obvious place was the secret room in the basement. But Kaitlyn couldn't get in that; Lewis had always used PK to find the hidden spring in the panel. Another place was in Mr. Z's house in San Francisco, where he'd kept it before. But Kaitlyn couldn't do anything about that today. Sometime she'd have to find a way to get to San Francisco.

For now . . . well, Joyce hadn't wanted her to see the testing. So Kait would start with the labs.

The front lab was as she remembered it, weird machines, a folding screen with seashells appliquéd on it, chairs and couches, bookcases, a stereo. There was no graffiti. Kaitlyn looked briefly into each of the study carrels that lined the walls, but she knew already that the crystal could never fit into something so small. She found only more equipment.

I wonder what their powers are? she thought, envisioning each of the students she'd met. I forgot to ask Lydia. Gabriel said something about Frost being clairvoyant, but the others—I'll bet they do something *bizarre*.

She turned to the back lab . . . and found it locked. A*ha!*

It had never been locked before. Kaitlyn found it extremely suspicious that it should be locked now.

But her jubilation changed to despair a minute later as she realized a basic truth. If it was locked, she *couldn't get in.*

But wait, wait. Joyce had always kept a house key on top of the bulletin board in the kitchen, for anybody to grab when they were leaving the house. Sometimes people had the same locks on the inside doors of a house as the outside. If that key were still there . . . and if it fit . . .

In a moment she was in the quiet, darkening kitchen, fingers searching anxiously on the top of the bulletin board's frame. She found some dust, a dead fly . . . and a key.

Eureka! Praying all the way, Kaitlyn hurried back to the lab. She held key to lock, almost dropping it in her nervousness.

It's *got* to work, it's *got* to work. . . .

The key slipped in. It fit! She waggled it. It turned!

The doorknob turned, too. Kait pushed and the door was open. She stepped in and shut the door behind her.

The back lab was dim—it had been a garage and had only a small window. Kaitlyn blinked, trying to make out shapes. She didn't dare turn on a light.

There were bookcases here, too, and more equipment. And a steel room like a bank vault.

A Faraday cage.

Kaitlyn remembered Joyce telling her about it. It was for complete isolation in testing. Soundproof, electronically shielded. They had put Gabriel in there.

Kait remembered herself begging Joyce to promise *she'd* never have to go in.

Her mouth was dry. She tried to swallow, but her throat seemed to stick together. She walked toward the gray bulk of the steel vault, one hand lifted as if she were blind.

Cool metal met her fingers.

If I were a crystal, I'd be somewhere like this. Shielded, enclosed. With enough room for everybody to get in and crowd around me.

Kaitlyn's fingers slid over the metal. Her former tranquility in the face of danger was gone, and her heart wasn't just pounding, it was *thundering*. If the crystal was really in there, she had to see it. But she didn't really want to see it—and to be alone with that obscene thing . . . in the dark. . . .

Kaitlyn's skin was crawling and her knees felt unsteady. But her fingers kept searching. She found something like a handle.

You can do it. You can do it.

She pulled.

At first, she thought the sound she heard was the vault door clicking. Then she realized it was somebody opening the lab door behind her.

6

What does a spy do when she's caught?

Kait's stomach plummeted. She recognized the voice, even before she whirled around to see the figure silhouetted in the door.

Light shone behind him. Broad shoulders, then body lines that swept straight down. A man wearing a greatcoat.

"Are you finding anything to interest you?" Mr. Zetes asked, his gold-headed cane swinging in his hand.

Oh, God. The buzzing was back in Kaitlyn's ears and she couldn't answer. Couldn't move, either, although her heart was shaking her body.

"Would you like to see what's inside there?"

Say something, idiot. Say anything, *anything*.

Her dry lips moved. "I—no. I—I was just—"

Mr. Zetes stepped forward, snapped on the overhead light. "Go on, take a closer look," he said.

But Kaitlyn couldn't look away from his face. The first time she'd seen this man, she'd thought him courtly and aristocratic. His white hair, aquiline nose, and piercing dark eyes made him look like some English earl. And if an occasional grim smile flashed across his face, she was sure that he had a heart of gold underneath.

She'd found out differently.

Now, his eyes held her with an almost hypnotic power. Boring into her mind, gnawing. He looked more telepathic than Gabriel. His measured, imperious voice seemed to resound in her blood.

"Of course you want to see it," he said, and Kaitlyn's throat closed on her protests. He advanced on her slowly and steadily. "Look at it, Kaitlyn. It's a very sturdy Faraday cage. Look."

Against her will, Kaitlyn's head turned.

"It's natural that you would be interested in it—and in what's inside. Have you seen that yet?"

Kaitlyn shook her head. Now that she wasn't looking into those eyes, she found she could speak—a little. "Mr. Zetes—I wasn't—"

"Joyce told me that you had come back to join us." Mr. Z's voice was rhythmic . . . almost soothing. "I was very pleased. You have great talents, you know, Kaitlyn. And a keen, inquiring mind."

As he spoke he unlocked the vault with a key, grasped the handle. Kaitlyn was speechless again with fear. Please, she was thinking. Please, I don't want to see, just let me go.

"And now your curiosity can be satisfied. Go in, Kaitlyn."

He pulled the steel door open. There was a single lamp inside, the battery-driven kind that clamps on walls. It gave enough light for Kaitlyn to see the object below.

Not the crystal. A sort of tank, made of dark metal.

Bewildered, forgetting herself, Kaitlyn took a step forward. The tank was almost like a Dumpster trash can, except that instead of being rectangular it had one side which slanted steeply. A door was set in that steeply slanting side. It looked like the door to a hurricane cellar, leading down.

There were all sorts of pipes, cables, and hoses attached to the tank. One machine beside it looked like the electroencephalograph Joyce had used to measure Kaitlyn's brain waves. There were other machines Kaitlyn didn't recognize.

The tank itself felt like a giant economy-size coffin.

"What . . . is it?" Kaitlyn whispered. Dread was clogging her chest like ice. The thing gave off an aura of pure evil.

"Just a piece of testing equipment, my dear," Mr. Zetes said. "It's called an isolation tank. The ultimate Ganzfeld cocoon. Put a subject inside, and she is surrounded by perfect darkness and perfect silence. No light or sound can penetrate. It's filled with water, so she can't feel the effects of gravity or her own body. There is no sensory stimulation of any kind. Under those conditions, a person—"

Would go insane, Kaitlyn thought. She recoiled from the tank violently, turning away. Just the idea of it, to be abandoned in utter darkness and silence, was making her physically sick.

Mr. Z's hand caught her, holding her lightly but firmly. "Would be undistracted by outside influences, free to extend her psychic powers to the fullest. Just as you did when Joyce blindfolded you, my dear. Do you remember that?"

He had turned to look at her, holding her terrified gaze with his. She hadn't missed his use of personal pronouns. Put a subject inside and *she* can't feel *her* own body.

"As I said earlier, you have very great talents, Kaitlyn. Which I would like to see developed to their fullest."

He was pulling her toward the tank.

And she couldn't resist. That measured voice, that precise grip . . . she had no will of her own.

"Have you heard of the Greek concept of *arete,* my dear?" He had put aside his cane and was opening the hurricane-cellar door. "Self-actualization, becoming all you can be." He was pushing her toward the open door. "What do you think you can be, Kaitlyn?"

A black hole gaped in front of her. Kaitlyn was going into it.

"Mr. Zetes!"

The voice was thin and distant in Kaitlyn's ears. All she could see was the hole.

"Mr. Zetes, I didn't realize you were here. What are you doing?"

The pressure on Kait's neck eased and she could move of her own volition again. She turned and saw Joyce in the doorway. Gabriel and Lydia were behind her.

Then Kaitlyn simply stood, blinking and trying to breathe. Mr. Z was going over to Joyce, talking to her in an undertone. Kaitlyn saw Joyce look up at her in surprise, then shake her head.

"I'm sorry, but there's no help for it," Mr. Z said, with mild regret, as if saying "I'm sorry, but we'll have to cut expenses."

He's talking about my imminent demise, Kaitlyn realized, and suddenly she was talking, gabbling.

"Joyce, I'm sorry. I know I shouldn't have gone

inside here, but I wanted to see what changes you'd made, and there was nobody around to ask, and—I'm *sorry*. I didn't mean anything by it."

Joyce looked at her, hesitated, then nodded. She beckoned Mr. Z into the front lab and began talking to him. Kaitlyn followed slowly, warily.

She couldn't hear everything, but what she heard stopped her breath. Joyce was defending her, championing her to Mr. Z.

"The Institute can use her," Joyce said, her tanned face earnest—and strained with what looked like repressed desperation. "She's well-balanced, conscientious, reliable. Unlike the rest of—" She broke off. "She'll be an asset."

And Gabriel was agreeing.

"I can vouch for her," he said. Kaitlyn felt a surge of gratitude—and admiration for his level, dispassionate gray eyes. "I've probed her mind and she's sincere."

Even Lydia was chiming in—after everyone else, of course.

"She *wants* to be here—and I want her for my roommate. Please let her stay."

Listening to it, Kaitlyn was almost convinced herself. They all sounded so *sure*.

And somehow it worked—or seemed to work. Mr. Z stopped shaking his head regretfully and looked thoughtful. At last he shifted his jaw, drew a deep breath, and nodded.

"All right, I'm willing to give her a chance," he said. "I'd like to see a little more penitence in her—some signs of remorse—but I trust your judgment, Joyce. And we could certainly use another remote-viewer." He turned to give Kaitlyn a benevolent smile. "You and Lydia go along to dinner. I want a word with Gabriel."

It's over, Kaitlyn realized. They're not going to kill me; they're going to feed me. Her heart was only beginning to return to its normal rate. She tried to hide the trembling in her legs as she followed Lydia.

But it slowed her down, and before she could get out of the front lab she heard Mr. Z speak to Joyce again.

"Give her a chance, but watch her. And have Laurie Frost watch her, too. She's intuitive; she'll pick up on anything subversive. And if she finds something . . . you know what to do."

A sigh from Joyce. "Emmanuel . . . you know what I think about your 'final solution'—"

"We'll send her out on a job soon. That ought to prove something."

"Kait, are you coming?" Lydia called from the kitchen.

Kait went through the door, but dawdled on the other side. Mr. Z was speaking again.

"Gabriel, I'm afraid you've been careless."

Gabriel's voice was restrained but defiant. "About the shard? You haven't heard—"

"Not about that," Mr. Zetes said in his unhurried way. "Joyce explained that to me. But there was a man found half-dead on Ivy Street. He had all the signs of someone drained of life energy. The police have been making inquiries."

"Oh."

"*Very* careless of you to do that in our own neighborhood—and the man might talk." Mr. Z's voice dropped to an icy whisper. "Next time, *finish the job.*"

Kaitlyn was shivering when Gabriel came through

the door. She was barely able to give him a smile of gratitude.

Thanks.

He shrugged. *No problem.*

Dinner started off quietly. Joyce served bacon cheeseburgers, fare that never would have been allowed in the old days. The psychics eyed Kaitlyn from around the long table, but didn't say much. Kait had the feeling they were biding their time.

"So where was everybody this afternoon?" she asked Lydia, trying for normalcy.

"I was in Marin. Riding lessons," Lydia said in subdued tones—she never seemed to talk loudly around the other students.

"I was asleep," Gabriel said lazily.

No one else answered, including Joyce, who returned to the kitchen. Kaitlyn dropped the subject and ate fries. It was interesting, though—the ones who'd been out were also the ones who would have been involved in testing. Could they have been in San Francisco? In Mr. Z's house—with the crystal?

She made a mental note to follow up on the question.

What Joyce said next might have been coincidence. "So you've seen the isolation tank."

Kaitlyn almost inhaled a fry. "Yes. Have—has anybody really been in that thing?"

"Sure, it's cool," Bri said. She shut her eyes and leaned her head back. "Cosmic, man! Groooovy." Her expression of ecstasy was marred by the fact that her open mouth was full of half-chewed hamburger.

"Shut your face, you slut!" Frost snapped, flicking a pickle chip at her.

"Who's a slut, you bimbo?" Bri returned cordially, chewing. "Jimbo bimbo. Mumbo jumbo."

They both laughed: Frost shrilly, Bri gruffly.

Jackal Mac glared. "Quit with the freakin' noise," he said brutally. "You make me sick with that freakin' noise." He had been eating with fervent single-mindedness, the way Kaitlyn imagined a coyote might eat.

"I like to see girls have a good time," Renny said. He was eating with finicky precision, gesturing with a french fry. "Don't you, Mac?"

"You making fun of me? You making fun of *me,* man?"

Kaitlyn blinked. It was a non sequitur; she didn't follow Mac's logic. But it didn't take logic to read the sudden fury in his slitted eyes.

He stood up, towering over the table, leaning across to stare at Renny. "I said, you makin' fun of *me?*" he bellowed.

Renny let him have it with a hamburger in the face.

Kaitlyn gaped. The hamburger had been dripping with ketchup and Thousand Island dressing. Renny had thoughtfully removed the bun, so Jackal Mac got the full benefit of the condiments.

Bri shrieked with laughter. "What a pitch, what a pitch! Pitch, snitch!"

"Think that's *funny?*" Jackal Mac seized her by the hair and slammed her face into her plate. He began to grind it around and around. The giggles turned to screams.

Kaitlyn was now gasping. Frost plunged her long nails into a bowl of coleslaw and came out with a juicy handful. She threw it at Mac, but it scattered over the table, hitting Renny, too.

Renny seized a bottle of Clearly Canadian water— the fizzy kind.

"Time to go." Gabriel caught Kaitlyn by the arm

above the elbow and neatly lifted her from the chair out of the way of a burst of carbonated water. Lydia was already scuttling out of the room.

"But he's going to kill her!" Kaitlyn gasped. Mac was still grinding Bri's face into the plate.

"So?" Gabriel piloted her toward the kitchen.

"No, I mean, *really*. I think that plate cracked; he's going to *kill* her."

"I said, 'so?' "

There was the sound of shattering glass and Kaitlyn looked back. Jackal Mac had stopped grinding Bri's face; Renny was now slashing at him with a broken Clearly Canadian bottle.

"Oh, my *God*—"

"Come on."

In the kitchen, Joyce was washing dishes.

"Joyce, they're—"

"It happens every night," Joyce said shortly. "Leave it alone."

"Every night?"

Gabriel stretched, looking bored. Then he smiled. "Let's go up to my balcony," he said to Kaitlyn. "I need some air."

"No, I—I want to help Joyce with the dishes." There was no point in trying to deceive him about such a minor thing, so she added, *I want to talk to her a minute. I didn't have time earlier.*

"Suit yourself." Gabriel's voice was unexpectedly cold; his expression was stony. "I'll be busy later." He left.

Kaitlyn didn't understand why he was angry, but there was nothing to do about it. She was a spy, she had information to gather. Picking up a dish, she said abruptly, "Joyce, why do you put up with it?"

"With Gabriel? I don't know, why do you?"

"With *them.*" Kaitlyn jerked her chin toward the dining room, where yells and crashes could still be heard.

Joyce gritted her teeth and scrubbed viciously at a greasy pan with a soap pad. "Because I have to."

"No really. Everything's so crazy now—and it seems like it's against everything you believe in." Kaitlyn was getting incoherent—maybe the scare before dinner was still affecting her. She had the feeling that she should shut up, but instead she blundered on. "I mean, you seem like the kind of person who really *believes* in things, and I just don't understand—"

"You want to know why? I'll show you!" With a soapy hand, Joyce seized something that had been on the counter, underneath the Chinese take-out containers.

It was a magazine, the *Journal of Parapsychology.*

"My name is going to be in this! The lead article. And not just this." Joyce's face was contorted, it reminded Kaitlyn of the way she'd looked when she'd held Gabriel's bleeding forehead against the crystal, trying to kill him. Overcome by maniacal passion.

"Not just this, but in *Nature, Science, The American Journal of Psychology, The New England Journal of Medicine,*" Joyce raved. "Multidisciplinary journals, the most prestigious journals in the world. My name and my work."

Dear God, she's a mad scientist, Kaitlyn thought. She was almost spellbound by the ranting woman.

"And that's just the beginning. Awards. Grants. A full professorship at the school of *my* choice. And, incidentally, a little trinket called the Nobel Prize."

Kait thought at first that she was joking. But there was no humor in those glazed aquamarine eyes. Joyce looked as insane as any of the psycho psychics.

Could he have hit her with the crystal, too? Kaitlyn wondered dazedly. Or could it be some sort of cumulative effect from being around it, like secondhand smoke?

But she knew that no matter what the crystal had done to warp and magnify the desire, it was Joyce's desire in the first place. Kaitlyn had finally discovered what made Joyce run; she had just seen into the woman's soul.

"That's why I put up with it, and why I'm going to put up with anything. So that the cause of science can be advanced. And so I can get *what I'm due.*"

As suddenly as she had grabbed it, Joyce dropped the magazine she'd been shaking in front of Kaitlyn's eyes. She turned back to the sink.

"Now, why don't you take a walk," she said in a voice suddenly gone dull. "I can wash the dishes by myself."

Numb, Kaitlyn walked out of the kitchen. She avoided the dining room, went through the front lab and up the stairs.

Gabriel's door was locked. Well, she should have expected that, really. She'd managed to offend two of the three people who'd championed her tonight. Might as well try for a perfect score, she thought philosophically, and headed for the room she was to share with Lydia.

But Lydia proved to be impossible to offend or talk to at all. She was in bed with the covers pulled over her head. Whether she was sulking or simply scared, Kaitlyn didn't know. She wouldn't come out.

So *moody,* Kaitlyn thought.

It was a very long, very dull evening. Kait listened to the other psychics stagger up to their various rooms, then a TV blared from one room, a stereo from the other. It spoiled Kaitlyn's concentration for the one thing that might have relaxed her: drawing.

And this room depressed her. All her possessions had disappeared from it—thrown away when the new students came in. Anna's raven mask was lying in a corner. Like a piece of garbage. Kait didn't dare hang it up where it belonged.

Finally, she decided to take a bath and follow Lydia's example. She had a long soak, curled up in bed—and then there was nothing to do but think.

Scenes from the day kept floating through her mind. The face of the red-haired man . . . Gabriel's face in the dawn light. Mr. Z's silhouette.

I've got to make plans, she thought. Mysteries to investigate. Ways to find the crystal. But her mind couldn't focus on one thing, it kept skipping.

Joyce defended me . . . I fooled the fooler. And what convinced her was that Rob and I had broken up . . . because Rob liked Anna.

What an idea. How odd. And Gabriel fell for it, too.

She must be sleepy. Her mind skipped again, her thoughts becoming less and less cohesive. I hope Gabriel isn't really angry with me. I need him. Oh, God, all the things I said to him . . .

Was that wrong? To let him think I'm in love with him? But it wasn't completely a lie. I do care about him. . . .

As much as I do about Rob?

It was a heretical thought, and one which jerked her fully awake. She realized she had been half-dreaming.

But the thought wouldn't go away.

In Canada she had discovered that Gabriel loved

her. Loved her in a vulnerable, childlike way she could never have believed if she hadn't *seen* it, felt it in his mind. He had been completely open to her, so warm, so joyous . . .

. . . the way he was this morning, her mind whispered.

But in Canada she hadn't loved him. Or at least she hadn't been in love.

You couldn't be in love with two people at the same time. You *couldn't* . . .

Could you?

Suddenly Kaitlyn felt icy cold. Her hands were cold, her face was cold. As if someone had opened a window somewhere inside her and let a glacial wind blow in.

If I loved Gabriel . . . if I loved both of them . . .

How could I choose?

How could I choose?

The words were ringing so loudly in her head that she didn't notice the very real noise in her room. Not until a shadow loomed on the wall beside her.

Terror swept her. For an instant she thought it was Mr. Z—and then she saw Gabriel beside her bed.

Oh, Lord, did he hear my thought? She groped for shields, found she didn't have any. She was burned out.

But Gabriel was smiling, looking at her from under heavy eyelids. He would never have smiled like that if he had heard. "Ready to try out the balcony now?" he asked.

Kaitlyn looked at him, slowly regaining her composure. He was looking particularly gorgeous, and dangerous as darkness. She felt a magnetic pull drawing her to him.

But she was exhausted. Unshielded. And she had

just discovered a crisis within herself that threatened to bring the world crashing down.

I can't go with him. It would be insane.

The magnetic pull only got stronger. She wanted to be held. She wanted him to hold her.

"Come on," Gabriel whispered, and took her hand. He caressed the palm with his thumb. "Kiss me, Kait."

7

Kaitlyn was shaking her head at him. What on earth could the girl mean?

Gabriel could tell she wanted to come. He'd read the line in some old book somewhere, probably during one of his stints in solitary. "She trembled at his touch." Reading it, he'd sneered—but now he was seeing the real thing. When he reached down to take her hand, Kaitlyn trembled.

So what was the problem?

I'm tired, she projected in a whisper.

Oh, come on. Sitting on a balcony is relaxing.

He could tell she was going through some struggle. Mad because of the way he'd acted after dinner? Or . . .

Did it have something to do with what he'd seen this afternoon?

His mood darkened. *Is there something wrong?* he asked silkily.

"No, of course not," she said very quickly. On the

other bed a lump under the comforter stirred. Gabriel eyed it with distaste.

Kaitlyn was getting up. Gabriel's lip twitched at the sight of her nightgown—it was flannel and tentlike, covering her from throat to ankle. Quite a bit different from Frost, who had pirouetted in front of him dressed in what looked like a transparent red handkerchief the first night he'd met her. She'd made it clear, too, that she didn't mind if he took the handkerchief off.

Kaitlyn, by contrast, was holding the neck of her nightgown closed as she briskly walked to his room.

She paused there to look at the walls. "You do the graffiti?"

He snorted. *Mac. He was living here.*

"And what did he think when you asked him to get out?"

Gabriel said nothing, waited until she turned around. Then he gave her one of his most disturbing smiles. *I didn't ask.*

"Oh." She didn't pursue it. She stepped through the open sliding glass door onto the balcony. "It's a nice night," she murmured.

It was—a soft moonless night, with stars showing between branches of the olive trees. The air was warm, but Kaitlyn had her arms wrapped around herself.

Gabriel went still.

Maybe it was the simplest explanation after all. Maybe he'd been wrong about her trembling—or wrong about the reason. Not desire . . . but fear.

"Kaitlyn." Instinctively, he used words instead of thoughts, giving her the distance she seemed to need. "Kait, you don't have to . . . I mean, you *know* that, don't you?"

She turned quickly, as if startled. But then she didn't seem to know what to say. He could search her thoughts—he could sense them even now, like silver fish darting and gliding in clear water—but he *wouldn't*. He would wait for her to tell him.

She was staring at him, breathing lightly. "Oh, Gabriel. I do know. And I can't explain—I'm just . . . oh, it's been a hard day."

Then she put her hands over her face. She started to cry, with her hair falling around her, and little quick intakes of breath.

Gabriel stood transfixed.

Kaitlyn the indomitable—crying. She did it so seldom that he was too amazed at first to react. When he could move, he could think of only one thing to do.

He took her in his arms, and Kaitlyn clung to him. Clung tightly—and after a moment lifted a tear-stained face to him.

The kisses were soft and slow and very passionate. It was strange to do this without touching her mind, but he wasn't going to be the first to initiate contact. He'd wait for her. Meanwhile, it was a sort of pleasurable agony to restrain himself.

And it was good just to hold her and touch the softness of her skin. He wanted to hold her hard, not to hurt her but to keep her safe, to show her that he was strong enough to protect her. Her beauty was like fire and strange music, and he loved her.

And he *could* love her, because she didn't belong to anyone else, and she loved him back. She'd given it all up for him.

For an instant he felt a flicker of guilt at that, but it was swept aside by a fierce desire to hold her closer. To *be* closer. He couldn't keep himself in check any longer. He reached for her mind, a tendril of thought extending to caress her senses.

Kaitlyn recoiled. Not just pulling away from his mind, but pulling out of his arms. He could feel her trying to fling up shields against him.

Leaving him stricken, utterly bewildered, and bereft. Cold because she'd taken all the warmth in the universe away with her.

Suspicion knifed through him, unavoidable this time.

What is it you don't want me to see?

"Nothing!" She was frightened—no, panicked. His suspicion swelled until it was larger than both of them, until it blocked out everything else. He threw words at her like stones.

"You're lying! Don't you think I can tell?" He stared at her, controlling his breath, forcing his voice into velvety-iron tones. "It wouldn't have something to do with Kessler coming around here this afternoon, would it?"

"Rob—here?"

"Yeah. I felt his mind and tracked him down to the redwood trees out back. You're telling me you didn't know?"

Her eyes were still wide with surprise—but he saw, and felt, the flash of guilt. And his suspicions were confirmed.

"What are you really doing here, Kaitlyn?"

"I told you. I—"

"Stop lying to me!" Again he had to stop to control himself. When he spoke again his voice was like ice because he was made of ice. "You didn't break it off with him, did you? And you're not here to join us. You're a spy."

"That's not true. You won't even give me a chance—"

"I told them all that I'd seen into your mind—but I never really did. You made sure of that. You did a wonderful job of tricking me."

Her eyes were large and fierce with pain. "I didn't trick you," she said in a ragged voice. "And if you think I'm a spy, then why don't you go tell Joyce? Why don't you tell them all?"

He was calm, now, because a block of ice can't feel. "No, I won't do that. I'll let you do it to yourself. And you will, sooner or later—probably sooner, because the old man isn't stupid and Frost will pick things up. You'll betray yourself."

There was a blue flame of defiance in her eyes now. "I'm telling you, I am not a spy," she said.

"Oh, right. You're perfectly sincere. I believe you completely." Quick as a striking snake, he bent over her, thrusting his face close to hers. "That's fine, as long as you remember one thing. Keep out of my way. If you mess with *my* plans, angel—no mercy."

Then he left, stalking out of the room to be alone with his dark bitterness.

Kaitlyn cried herself to sleep.

"Bri—school! Frost—testing!"

The shouting voice in the hall woke Kaitlyn. She felt languid and stupid, with a stuffed-up nose and a bad headache.

The door banged open. "Lydia—school! Kaitlyn, you're going to school, too. I arranged it yesterday, and I'm coming in with you today."

Thanks for telling me, Kaitlyn thought, but she got up—painfully, because every muscle seemed to be aching. She stumbled to the bathroom and began to go through the routine of dressing like a programmed robot. Shower, first.

The warm water felt good on her upturned face, but her mind kept leaping back to what had happened with Gabriel last night. At first everything had been so wonderful—and then . . . it had hurt her to see his eyes like holes in his face and his mouth tight to keep it from working.

You ought to be glad it all turned awful, a voice inside her whispered. Because if it had stayed good— well, what would you do? What would you do about Rob?

She didn't *know* what she would have done. Her entire middle was a tight ball of anguish and she was so confused.

It didn't matter. Gabriel hated her now, anyway. And that was *good,* because she was going to be true to Rob. It was good—except for the minor fact that Gabriel might denounce her to Mr. Z and get her killed.

Tears mingled with the shower spray on her face. Kaitlyn turned her head aside to take a deep, shuddering breath, and that was why she didn't see the shower curtain being pulled open.

The first thing she knew was a rough hand closing around her wet arm.

"What do you think you're doing? Get out of there!" Bri shouted, adding a string of expletives. Kaitlyn had to step over the side of the tub or fall over it—she was being dragged out. Naked and stunned, she shook her hair back and stared at the other girl.

"You think you can use all the hot water again? Like you did last night?" That was the gist of what Bri was yelling, although actually every other word was a curse. Kaitlyn stood dripping on the tile floor, dumb-founded.

"You think you're better than us, don't you?" Bri shouted. "You're Little Miss Responsible, teacher's pet. You can use all the water you want to. You've never had it hard."

The sentences were disjointed, and again Kaitlyn had that sense of something being *off,* as if Bri couldn't actually get a fix on what was making her angry. But her anger and resentment were clear enough.

"Everybody's darling," she mocked, cocking her head back and forth, with a finger to her chin—a bizarre Shirley Temple impersonation. "Looks so *sweet*—"

Something snapped. Kaitlyn's temper had always been combustible, and now it ignited like rocket accelerant touched with a match. Naked as she was, she seized Bri and slammed her against a wall. Then she pulled her away and slammed her back again. Bri's mouth fell open and her eyes showed white. She fought, but fury gave Kaitlyn inhuman strength.

"You think I've always had things easy?" she yelled into Bri's face. "You don't know how it was back in Ohio. I was from the wrong side of the tracks anyway, but to top it off, *I was a witch.* You think I don't know what it's like to have people cross themselves when you look at them? When I was five the bus driver wouldn't take me to school—she said my mom ought to get me blessed. And then my mom died—"

Tears were sliding down Kaitlyn's cheeks, and she was losing her anger. She slammed Bri again and got it back.

"Kids at school would run up and touch me for a dare. And adults would get so nervous when I talked to them—Mr. Rukelhaus used to get a *twitch* in his eye. I grew up feeling like something that ought to be put in the zoo. Don't tell me I don't know what it's like. *Don't tell me!*"

She was winding down, her breath slowly calming. So was Bri's.

"You dye your hair blue and do stuff to look weird—but you're doing it yourself, and you can change it. I can't change my eyes. And I can't change what I am."

Suddenly embarrassed, Kaitlyn let go of Bri's arms and looked around for a towel.

"You're okay," Bri said in a voice Kaitlyn hadn't heard her use before. Not a sneering tough-girl voice. Kait looked around, startled.

"Yeah, you're okay. I thought you were a goody-goody wimp, but you're not. And I think your eyes are cool."

She looked more sane than she had since Kait had met her.

"I—well, thanks. Thank you." Kait didn't know whether to apologize or not; she settled for saying, "You can use the shower now."

Bri gave a friendly nod.

It's strange, Kait thought as Joyce drove her to school. Bri, Lydia, and Renny had gone in Lydia's car. It's strange, but for a while there she sounded just like Marisol. What was it Marisol said that first night? *You kids think you're so smart—so superior to everyone else.*

But we *didn't* think that; it was just Marisol's paranoia—a very particular kind of paranoia. Kaitlyn shot a look at Joyce under her eyelashes. And Joyce has that kind, too—thinking she isn't getting what she's due.

They *all* think the world is out to get them—that they're special and superior but everybody is persecuting them. Can the crystal do that?

If it can, it's no wonder they're out to get the world first.

Joyce checked her in to school, and Kaitlyn found herself going to the same classes she had when she'd come to the Institute. The teachers put her absence down as a vacation, which was mildly amusing. It was surrealistic, like being in a dream, to sit in British literature again, with all these kids whose lives were quiet and boring and completely safe. Who hadn't had *anything* happen to them in the last few weeks; who hadn't changed at all. Kaitlyn felt out of step with the whole world.

Watch it, kid. Don't *you* get paranoid.

At lunch several people asked her to sit with them. Not just one group, but two, called to her in the cafeteria. It was the sort of thing Kaitlyn had always dreamed about, but now it seemed trivial. She was looking for Lydia—she wanted to talk to that girl.

Lydia wasn't in evidence. Bri and Renny were off in a corner, bullying people and probably extorting lunch money. Kaitlyn wondered how their teachers dealt with them.

I'll look around by the tennis courts, she thought. Maybe Lydia's eating her lunch out there.

She was crossing in front of the PE building when she saw three people crowded in the doorway of the boy's locker room. They were looking out from behind the little wall that kept people from seeing in the open doors, and they seemed ready to duck back at any moment. The weird thing was that one of them was a girl. A girl with long dark braids . . .

And the tallest boy had hair that shone in the sun

like old gold. Kaitlyn's heart leaped into her mouth and choked her. She ran.

"Rob—you shouldn't be here," she gasped as she got behind the wall. And then she was hugging him hard, overcome by how dear and familiar and honest and loyal and safe he was. His emotions wide open— not icy and shielded. She could *feel* how much he cared for her, how glad he was that she was alive and unhurt.

"I'm fine," she said, pulling back. "Really. And I'm sorry for running away without telling you—and I don't know why you're not mad."

Lewis and Anna were crowding around her, smiling, patting her as if to make sure she was real. They were *all* so dear and good and forgiving. . . .

"We were *worried* about you," Anna said.

"We camped out yesterday near the Institute hoping you'd come out," Lewis said. "But you never did."

"No—and *you* can't do that ever again," Kait said shakily. "Gabriel saw you. I don't think anybody else did, thank God, but he's bad enough."

"We won't have to do it again," Rob said, smiling. "Because we've got you now. We'll take you with us—even though we don't exactly have a place to go yet. Tony's working on that."

Kait thought he had never looked so handsome. His eyes were amber-gold, clear and full of light like the summer sky. His face was full of trust and happiness. She could feel the radiant energy of his love.

"Rob . . . I can't." The change in his expression made her feel as if she'd hit an innocent child in the face.

"You can." Then, as she kept shaking her head: *"Why not?"*

"For one thing, if I disappear, they'll think I've

betrayed them and they'll do something to my father. I *know* they will; I feel it in Joyce. And for another thing—Rob, it's *working.* I've got them snowed. They believe I've come back to join them and I've already had a chance to look around the house." She didn't dare tell him what had come of that; she had the feeling that if Rob knew, she'd be slung over his shoulders caveman style, being carried out of San Carlos.

"But what are you looking for? Kait, *why* did you come back here?" Anna said.

"Couldn't you figure that out? I'm looking for the crystal."

Rob nodded. "I thought it was something like that. But you don't need to live there, Kait. We'll break in sometime; we'll find a way."

"No, you won't. Rob, there are *five* psychics there, besides Lydia and Joyce, and they're all crazy-paranoid. Literally. We need somebody on the inside, who can move around the house freely, and who can figure out what's going on. Because I don't just want to find the crystal, I want to find the way to destroy it. I need to know everybody's schedule, figure out a time when we can get to it with the shard. We can't just go running in some afternoon waving it over our heads. They'll slaughter us."

"We'll fight back," Rob said grimly, his jaw at its most stubborn.

"They'll still slaughter us. They're *loonies.* You haven't seen what they've done to the house—" Kaitlyn caught herself. Too much description of the danger—she was about to get slung over Rob's shoulder. She changed tracks fast. "But they trust me. This morning one of the girls said I was okay. And Joyce wants me around because the rest of them are so far into the twilight zone. So I think everything will work out—if you'll just please let me get on with it."

Rob took a long, deep breath. "Kaitlyn, I can't. It's just too dangerous. I'd rather walk in and fight it out with Gabriel myself—"

"I *know* you would." And that's just what you're *not* going to do, Kait thought. "But it's not just Gabriel—you haven't seen the others. There's a guy called Jackal Mac who's about eight feet tall and has a shaved head and muscles like a gorilla. And I don't even *know* what his psychic power is, but I know that they're all hopped up on the crystal. It makes them stronger, and it makes them crazier."

"Then I don't want you with them."

"I *have* to be. Someone has to be. Don't you see that?" Kaitlyn felt her eyes filling—they seemed to do that a lot these days—and then she decided to do something dishonorable. To use those tears. She let them come, and she asked Rob, "Don't you trust me?"

She could see how it hurt him. His own eyes had a suspicious shine, but he answered steadily, "You know I do."

"Then why won't you let me do this? Don't you think I'm capable enough?"

It was completely unfair, as well as being unkind. And it worked. Rob had to admit that he thought she was very capable. The only one of them who could pull such a thing off. He even had to admit, finally, that it was a thing that probably needed to be done.

"Then why won't you *let* me?"

Rob gave in.

"But we'll come back and check on you next Monday."

"It's too dangerous, even at school—"

87

"Don't push it, Kait," Rob said. "Either you let us check on you regularly or you don't stay at all. We'll be here on Monday at lunch. If you don't show up, we're coming in after you."

Kaitlyn sighed, knowing Rob wasn't going to budge. "Okay. And I'll call when I find the crystal and I know a time we can get to it. Oh, Lewis—I should have thought of this before. How do you make the secret panel slide back?"

Lewis's almond-shaped eyes widened in dismay. "Huh? Kait—I don't know!"

"Yes, you do. Something inside you knows, because you do it."

"But I can't say it in words—and besides, you don't have PK."

"Neither does Joyce or Mr. Z, and the panel was made for them. And if you can't say it in words, just think it to me. Just think *about* it and let me listen."

Lewis was reluctant and doubtful, but he screwed up his face and began to think. "I just sort of feel around with my fingers—I mean with my mind— behind the wood. Like this. And I feel something metallic here. And then when I get to about here . . ."

"It opens! So the springs or whatever have to be in those places. You're a good visual thinker; I can see just what parts of the panel you mean." Kait made a note of the images, freezing them in her memory as she hugged him. "Thanks, Lewis."

And I'll mention you to Lydia, she added soundlessly, because a picture of Lydia was running underneath all Lewis's other thoughts.

She felt his shy embarrassment, like a mental blush. *Thanks, Kait.*

Then she hugged Rob again. *I'm glad you came.*

Be careful, he sent back to her, and she wished she

could just go on hugging him, standing here and feeling safe. He was so good and she cared about him so much.

When she hugged Anna she projected a private message. *Take care of him for me—please?*

Anna nodded, biting her lip to keep the tears back. Kait left without looking behind her.

The rest of the school day was uneventful, but Kait felt exhausted. She was fumbling in her locker after the last bell rang, when Bri came running interference through the crowd.

"Hurry up," she said in her boyish voice. "Come on; Joyce is waiting for you. She sent me to get you."

"What's the rush?" Kait asked nervously. Bri's dark eyes were snapping; her cheeks were flushed with excitement.

"Black Lightning strikes! Mr. Zetes has a job for us."

8

Kait hurried toward Joyce's car with a knot in her stomach. She didn't know what kind of jobs Mr. Z had the kids do, but she knew she wasn't going to like it.

As it turned out, though, Joyce wasn't rushing them to the job. She was taking four of them shopping.

Gabriel, Renny, Frost, and Kaitlyn. They dropped Bri at the Institute where she stood on the sidewalk screaming with rage.

"It's not her fault, but she just doesn't look the part," Joyce said rather calmly as she headed for the freeway. "I told her not to put that blue in her hair."

Kaitlyn, squashed between Frost and Renny in the tiny backseat, felt as if she had lost her only friend. Not that she would rely on Bri, actually, or trust her as far as she could throw her. But the other three were openly hostile; Gabriel wasn't speaking to her, Renny kept whispering obscene suggestions in her ear, and

Frost gave her a spiteful pinch whenever she thought Joyce wouldn't notice.

"What part doesn't she look?" Kait asked faintly.

"You'll see." Joyce drove them to a mall and pulled up in front of Macy's. There she ensconced Gabriel and Renny in the men's department and hustled Kait and Frost to the women's. She pushed Kait past Liz Claiborne and into Anne Klein.

"Now we're going to find you each a suit. Tweed, I think. Brown, anyway. Very conservative, only a little slit in the skirt."

Kaitlyn didn't know whether to laugh or groan. She'd never had a suit before, so this should have been exciting—but tweed?

It wasn't so bad when she got it on. Joyce pulled her hair back and Kait eyed herself in the mirror thoughtfully. She looked very trim and serious, like the librarian in a movie who starts out with her hair in a bun and horn-rim glasses and then blossoms by the end of the picture.

Frost's transformation was even more amazing. Her normal attire was a style Kait had privately dubbed "slunge"—a cross between sleaze and grunge. But in a double-breasted brown wool suit, she looked like another librarian—from the neck down.

"When we get home, you'll lose the lipstick—all of it—and half the mascara," Joyce told her. "And you'll put that rat's nest into a French twist. Also lose the gum."

The boys were equally transmogrified by three-piece Mani suits and leather shoes. Joyce paid for everything and hustled them out of the store.

"When do you tell us what we're doing?" Gabriel asked in the car.

"You'll hear the details at home. But basically it's a burglary."

Kaitlyn's stomach knotted again.

"So what now?" Anna asked. They were sitting in a Taco Bell in Daly City. Tony had promised to find them a place to stay with one of his friends—an apartment in San Francisco. But he hadn't found the place yet, and Rob was worried about staying any longer at Tony's house. So they spent as much time as possible outdoors, where they might be hard to find.

For the first time since Kaitlyn had disappeared Rob had an appetite.

But he would never in a hundred years have imagined he'd have left her at the Institute. The little witch—he still wasn't quite sure how she'd persuaded him. Of *course,* she was capable, but even a capable person could easily get killed there.

She'd asked him to trust her, that was it. All right, then, by God, he'd trust her. It was hard to let her go—he didn't think anyone realized how hard. He would very much have preferred to go himself. But . . .

I believe in you, Kaitlyn Fairchild, he thought. Just please God keep yourself safe.

He was so deep in his own thoughts that Anna had to poke him and ask silently, *I said, what now, Rob?*

"Huh? Oh, sorry." He stopped sucking on his Coke, considered. "Well, we've been too busy watching Kait to take care of Marisol. I guess we'd better do that now. Tony said his parents wouldn't be at the hospital till tonight, so it's a good time."

"Should we get Tony to go with us?" Lewis asked.

Rob thought. "No, I guess not. If it doesn't work, it'll be pretty hard on him to watch. We'll find some way to make them let us in." Tony had warned them that Marisol wasn't allowed visitors, except family.

They drove to St. Luke's Hospital in San Francisco, and Rob took the crystal shard out of the glove compartment. It was a crazy place to keep it, but they had to take it with them wherever they went. He slipped it into the sleeve of his sweater—it was just about as long as his forearm—and they strolled into the hospital.

On the third floor Rob beckoned a nurse—"Ma'am? Could I ask you a question?"—and sweet-talked her while Lewis and Anna snuck in Marisol's room. Then when all the nurse's phones began to ring at once, he snuck in himself. The ringing was provided by Lewis's PK, a neat trick, in Rob's opinion.

Inside the room, he felt Anna's shock. She was trying bravely to conceal it, but it showed through. He squeezed her shoulder and she smiled at him gratefully, then she stopped smiling and moved away so abruptly that he was startled.

Upset, probably. Marisol looked bad. Rob remembered her as a vivid, handsome girl, all tumbled red-brown hair and full pouting lips. But now . . .

She was painfully thin. There were all sorts of tubes and wires and monitors attached to her. Her right arm was on top of the blanket, with the wrist cocked at an impossible angle, turned in against the forearm. And she *moved*—her head twisted constantly, writhing on her neck, her brown eyes partway open but unseeing. Her breathing was frightening to hear: She seemed to be sucking air in through clenched teeth as she grimaced.

I thought people in comas were quiet, Lewis thought shakily.

Rob knew better. He'd been in a coma himself, after meeting a mountain at fifty miles an hour. He'd been hang gliding at Raven's Roost off the Blue Ridge Parkway, and he'd hit wind shear and stalled out. He'd broken both arms, both legs, his jaw, enough ribs to puncture a lung . . . and his neck. A hangman's fracture—so called because it's the same place your neck breaks when they hang you. Nobody expected him to live, but a long while later he'd woken to find himself in a Stryker frame and his granddaddy crying.

He'd spent months in bed and during those months he'd discovered his powers. Maybe they'd been there all along, and he'd just never sat still long enough to notice them, or maybe they were a gift because God was sorry about smashing a li'l ol' farm boy into that mountain. Either way, it had changed his life, made him see what a dumb sucker he'd always been, how selfish and shortsighted. Before, he'd aspired to being a guard for the Blue Devils at Duke. After, he aspired to help some.

Now, he felt shame flood up to drown him. How could he have left Marisol like this a day longer than she needed to be? He shouldn't have waited, not even to watch out for Kait. There was no excuse for it—he was still a dumb sucker and a selfish jerk. Fat lot of help he'd given Marisol.

This time Anna squeezed *his* shoulder. *None of us realized,* she said. *And we don't even know if we can help her, now. But let's try.*

He nodded, strengthened by her gentle practicality. Then, with one glance up at a picture of the Madonna and Child above the bed, he pulled the crystal out of his sleeve. It was cold and heavy in his hand. He wasn't sure where to apply it—LeShan hadn't said anything about that. After some thought he gently touched it to her forehead, the site of the third eye. A powerful energy center.

And nothing happened.

Rob waited, and waited some more. The tip of the shard rested between lank strands of red-brown hair. Marisol's head kept twisting. There was no change in her energy level.

"It's not working," Lewis whispered.

Fear pricked at Rob like tiny hornet stings. Was it his fault? Had he left it too long?

Then he thought, maybe the crystal needs a little help.

He took a deep breath, shut his eyes, and concentrated.

He never could explain exactly how he did his healing—how he knew what to do. But somehow he could feel what was wrong with a person. He could see different kinds of energy running through them like bright-colored rivers—and sometimes not flowing, but dark and stagnant, stuck. Marisol was almost all stuck. There was some sort of blockage between brain and body, and nothing was flowing either way.

How to fix that? Well, maybe start with the third eye, send energy through the crystal until it pushed hard enough against the plugs to blow them free.

Gold energy, flooding down the crystal. The crystal swirled it in a spiral and amplified it, heightening it with every turn. So that was how this thing worked!

More energy. More. Keep it flowing. He could see it flowing into Marisol, now, or at least trying to. Her third eye was stopped up as if somebody had wedged a cork in there. The energy built up behind it, roiling and gold and getting hotter by the minute. Rob felt sweat break out on his forehead. It dripped into his eyes and burned.

Ignore it. Send more energy. More, more.

Rob was breathing hard, a little frightened by what was happening. The energy was a crackling, spinning mass now, so hot and dense that he could barely hold onto the crystal. It was like trying to control a high-pressure fire hose. And trying to send more energy in was like trying to pump air into a critically overinflated bicycle tire. Something had to give.

Something did. Like a cork blowing out of a bottle, the blockage flew out of Marisol's third eye. The force of the energy behind it chased it down her body and out the soles of her feet almost faster than Rob's eye could follow.

Gold everywhere. Marisol's entire body was encased in gold as the energy raced around, rushing through veins and capillaries, circulating at a wildly accelerated speed. An internal whirlpool bath. God, it was going to kill the girl. Nobody was meant to have that much energy.

Rob jerked the crystal away from her forehead.

Marisol's body had been straining, her back arching as the energy shot through her. Now she fell back and lay completely still for the first time since they'd walked in. Her eyes were shut. Rob realized suddenly that one of her monitors was blaring like an alarm going off.

Then, as he watched, her right hand began to move. The fingers unclenched, the wrist relaxed. It looked like a normal hand again.

"Oh, God," Lewis whispered. "Oh, look at that."

Rob couldn't speak. The alarm went on blaring. And Marisol's eyes opened.

Not halfway. All the way. Rob could see the intelligence in them. He reached out to touch her cheek, and she blinked and looked scared.

"It's okay," he told her, loud over the alarm. "You're going to be all right, you understand?"

She nodded uncertainly.

Running footsteps sounded outside the door. A sturdy nurse burst in, got almost to the bed before she skidded and saw Rob.

"What do you think you're doing in here? Did you touch anything?" she demanded, hands on hips—and then she took a good look at Marisol.

"Ma'am, I think she's feeling a little better," Rob said, and smiled because he couldn't help it.

The nurse was looking from Marisol to the monitors. She broke into a huge grin, switched the monitor off, and took Marisol's pulse.

"How're you feeling, darlin'?" she asked with tears shining in her eyes. "You just hang on one minute so I can get Doctor Hirata. Your mama's going to be so happy." Then she rushed out of the room without yelling at Rob.

"I think we'd better go before Doctor Hirata gets here," Lewis whispered. "He might ask some awkward questions."

"You're right." Rob grinned at Marisol, touched her cheek again. "I'll tell your brother you're awake, okay? And he'll be over here as fast as he can drive. And your parents, too . . ."

"Rob," Lewis whispered urgently.

They made it to the back stairs without being caught. On the second landing they stopped and whacked each other in glee.

"We did it!" Rob whispered, his voice echoing in the empty stairwell. "We did it!"

"You did it," Anna said. Her dark eyes were glowing and wise. It wasn't true, it had been the crystal, but

her praise made Rob feel warm to the tips of his fingers.

He hugged Lewis and felt happy. Then he hugged Anna and felt a surge of something different from what he felt for Lewis. Stronger . . . warmer.

It confused him. He'd only felt something like it once before—when he'd found Kaitlyn alive down in Mr. Z's basement. It was almost like pain in its intensity, but it wasn't pain.

Then he pulled back, shocked and mortified. How could he let himself feel like that about anyone but Kaitlyn? How could he let himself feel even a little like that?

And he knew Anna could tell, and that she was upset, because she wouldn't meet his eyes and she was holding herself shielded. She was disgusted with him, and no wonder.

Well, one thing was for certain. It would never happen again, never.

They walked down the rest of the stairs with only Lewis talking.

"All right, this is the place," Gabriel said. It was an imposing stone building on a one-way street in the financial district of San Francisco. Through the metal-framed glass doors Kait could see a guard at a little booth.

"Joyce said the guard won't give us any trouble. We sign in with the names she told us. The law firm is Digby, Hamilton, and Miles, the floor is sixteen."

He didn't look at Kaitlyn as he spoke and he didn't glance at her as they went inside. She didn't seem to exist for him anymore. But Joyce had told them to go in pairs, and Kait was supposed to walk by Gabriel.

She tried to do it without showing any more expression than he did.

The guard was wearing a red coat and talking on a cellular phone. He barely looked at them as Gabriel flipped through papers on a clipboard. Gabriel signed, and then it was Kait's turn. She wrote *Eileen Cullen, Digby, Hamilton, and Miles, 16,* and *11:17,* on the appropriate lines. The 11:17 was the "Time In."

Frost and Renny signed in and they crossed the tile mosaic floor to a bank of brass elevators. A man in jeans was polishing the brass, and Kaitlyn stared at her neat brown Amalfi shoes while they waited—it seemed a long time—for the elevator.

Once inside, Gabriel pushed a large black button for floor sixteen. The button stuck. The elevator started, slowly, and with a wheeze.

Renny was snickering and Frost let out a torrent of gasping giggles.

"Do you know what I signed for my name?" Renny asked, banging the elevator door. "I signed Jimi Hendrix. And I put for the company, Dewey, Cheatum, and Howe. Get it? Dewey, Cheatum, and Howe for a law firm!"

"And I put Ima Pseudonym," Frost said, tittering.

Kaitlyn's heart gave a violent thud and began racing. She stared at them, appalled. They *looked* normal now: Frost's hair was pulled back elegantly and she was wearing only one earring in each ear and Renny could have been a junior accountant. But underneath they were still the same raving loonies.

"Are you guys *nuts?*" she hissed. "If that guard takes a look at that sheet—oh, God, or if the next person who signs in just *glances* up—we are *dead. Dead.* How could you do such a thing?"

Renny just waved a hand at her, weak with laughter. Frost sneered.

Kait turned to Gabriel to share her horror. It was a reflex—she should have known better. However horrified he might have been a minute ago, he now shrugged and flashed a quick, mocking smile.

"Good one," he said to Renny.

"I knew *you* had a sense of humor," Frost purred, running a silvery fingernail up Gabriel's gray wool sleeve. She ran it all the way to his crisp white collar, then toyed with the dark hair behind his ear.

Kaitlyn gave her a blistering glare through narrowed eyes. Then she stared at the elevator buttons, fuming silently. She didn't like this job. She *still* hadn't been told what they were doing—what can you burglarize in a law firm? She didn't even know what psychic powers Frost and Renny had. And now she had to worry about what other insane things they might decide to do.

The elevator doors opened.

"What a dump," Renny said, and snickered. Gabriel cast an appreciative look around. The walls were paneled in some beautiful reddish gold wood and the floor was dark green marble. Through glass doors Kait could see what looked like a conference room.

Gabriel glanced at the map Joyce had given him. "Now we go right."

They passed rest room doors—even those looked opulent—and entered a hallway with dark green carpeting. They stopped when they came to a set of doors blocking their way. The doors were very big and heavy; they looked like metal, but when Kaitlyn touched one it was wood. And locked.

"This is it," Gabriel said. "Okay, Renny."

But Renny was gone. Frost, standing a little way

back, said, "He had to go to the little boys' room." She was struggling to keep a straight face.

Kaitlyn clenched her fists. She'd seen the graffiti at the Institute; she could just bet what he was doing in there. "Now what?" she snarled at Gabriel. "Look, are you going in there to get him, or am I?"

Gabriel ignored her, but she could see the tightness of his jaw. He started toward the bathroom, but at that moment Renny came out, his face the picture of innocence.

"I would have thought," Gabriel said without looking at Kait, "that you'd be happy if we screwed this up. After all, you're not really one of us . . . are you?"

Kaitlyn felt chilled. "I am, even if you don't believe it," she said, working to put sincerity in her voice. "And maybe I don't like stealing things, but I don't want to get caught and sent to jail, either." As Renny approached, walking cockily, she added in an undertone, "I don't even know why we *brought* him."

"Then watch and see," Gabriel said tersely. "Renny, this is it. From here on you need a security pass."

The device on the wall looked vaguely familiar. It was like the machines at the gas station that you slide a credit card through to charge gas automatically.

"Yeah, magnetic," Renny muttered. He pushed his glasses back with an index finger on the nosepiece and ran a hand over the security pass reader. "Anybody looking?" he said.

"No, but do it fast," Gabriel replied.

Renny stroked the device again and again. His face was wrinkled up, monkeylike. Kaitlyn chewed her lip and watched the central area from which they'd just come. Anybody stepping out of an elevator would see them.

"There you are, baby," Renny whispered suddenly. And the right hand door swung open.

So now Kaitlyn knew. Renny had PK, psychokinesis; he could move objects by power of mind alone. Including the little mechanisms inside security pass readers, apparently.

Just like Lewis, Kaitlyn thought. I wonder if there's something about short guys.

The door closed behind them when they went through.

Gabriel led them quickly down the hallway. On the left other hallways branched away; on the right were secretaries' carrels with computers on the desks. Behind the carrels were office doors, with names on brass nameplates beside them. Kaitlyn saw one nameplate that said WAR ROOM.

Maybe law is more exciting than I thought.

They came to another set of the big doors and Renny dealt with them in the same way. They walked down another hallway.

The farther they got into private territory, the more frightened Kait was. If anyone caught them here, they would have some explaining to do. Joyce hadn't given them any advice about that—Kaitlyn had the sick feeling that Gabriel might be expected to use his power.

"What are we *looking* for, anyway?" Kait whispered to Gabriel between her teeth. "I mean, have they got the Mona Lisa here or something?"

"Keep your stupid mouth shut. Anyone walking up one of those hallways could hear us."

Kaitlyn was stunned into silence. Gabriel had never spoken to her like that before. And he hadn't said a word about Renny and Frost doing really dangerous things.

She blinked and set her teeth, determined not to speak again, no matter what.

"This is it," Gabriel said at last. The nameplate on the door said E. Marshall Winston. "Locked," Gabriel said. "Renny, open it. Everybody else keep your eyes out. If anybody sees us here, we've had it."

9

Kaitlyn stared down the hall until she saw red afterimages. She was sweating onto her white silk blouse. Then she heard a snap and the door opened.

"Frost, keep watching out. Renny, come with me."

Kaitlyn felt sure Gabriel wanted her to keep watching, too, but couldn't bring himself to name her. She followed Renny into the dark office. Gabriel was pulling the shades, cutting out the night.

"She said Mr. Z thought it would probably be in the file cabinet—I guess that's this." He went over to a wooden credenza with file drawers built in. "Locked."

Renny took care of that, while Gabriel shone a penlight on the drawers. Kaitlyn's heart was thumping, quick and hard. She was watching a crime being committed—a serious, major crime. And if they got caught, she was as guilty as any of the others.

Renny stepped back and Gabriel pulled the top file drawer out. Then he cursed softly, closed it, and pulled out the lower one.

It was crammed with hanging files in green folders,

each one neatly labeled. Kaitlyn watched the penlight illuminate labels: Taggart and Altshuld—Reorganization. Star Systematics—Merger. Slater Inc.— Liquidation. TCW—Refinancing.

"Yes!" Gabriel whispered. He pulled out the thick hanging file that said TCW.

Inside were a lot of manila folders. Gabriel began going through them deftly. It all seemed to be paper, mostly white paper covered with courier type, a few booklets with paper as thin as Bible pages.

In a strange way, Kaitlyn felt relieved. It didn't seem so wrong to steal paper, even if it was important paper. It wasn't like taking money or jewels.

Gabriel's breath hissed out.

He was peering into a manila envelope. He pulled out the papers inside it, scattering them on the credenza's flat top, and shone the light on them.

Kaitlyn squinted, trying to make out what they were. They looked like certificates or something, heavy blue-gray paper, with a fancy border around the edges.

Then her eyes focused on tiny words Gabriel was tracing with his finger. Pay to Bearer . . .

Oh, my *God*.

Kaitlyn stood paralyzed, the print swimming before her eyes. She kept staring at the number on the bond, sure it couldn't be right, but it kept saying the same thing.

U.S. $1,000,000.

One million dollars.

And there were lots of the things. A pile of them.

Gabriel was flipping through, counting under his breath. "Twenty," he said at last. "That's right." He gathered the bonds up in his hands and caressed them. He was wearing the same expression Kaitlyn had seen when they toured Mr. Z's mansion. Like Scrooge counting his gold pieces.

Kaitlyn forgot her vow not to speak. "We're stealing twenty million dollars?" she whispered.

"A drop in the bucket," Gabriel said, and caressed the bonds again. Then he straightened up and began to briskly put the other folders back into the drawer. "We don't want a custodian or somebody to see anything's wrong tonight. Not until we get out of the building."

When the drawer was shut, he put the manila envelope inside his jacket. "Let's go."

Nobody was in the hall and they passed the first set of doors safely. From this side, the doors just pushed open. Kaitlyn didn't know whether to be nauseated or relieved. They were committing a felony. Gabriel was walking around with twenty *million* stolen dollars against his chest. And the horrible thing was that they were getting away with it.

Of course, on the brighter side, they were getting away with it. Kaitlyn wasn't going to jail.

That was when the two men stepped out of an office in front of them.

Kaitlyn's heart jumped into her mouth and then *burst.* Her feet were rooted to the floor and her hands and arms were numb. Her chest was squeezed so tightly that there was no room for her lungs to breathe.

Still, at first she thought the men wouldn't look her way. They did. Then she thought they wouldn't keep looking, wouldn't stare—because surely she was frightened *enough,* she'd been punished enough already. She wanted nothing to do with a life of crime.

But the men kept looking, and then the men were walking toward Kaitlyn's group. And then their mouths were moving. That was all Kaitlyn could take in at first, that the mouths were moving. She couldn't hear what they were saying, everybody seemed to be underwater or in a dream.

But a minute later her mind ran it all back for her, sharp and clear. "What are you doing here? You're not interns."

And there was suspicion in the voices, or at least a sense of wrongness. And Kaitlyn knew that if somebody didn't come up with something quick, that suspicion was going to harden and gel and they'd be trapped like flies in amber.

Think, girl. Think, *think.*

But for once, absolutely nothing came to her. Her quick brain was useless. All she could think of was the lump under Gabriel's black-flecked gray jacket, which was starting to look as big as an elephant inside a boa constrictor.

That was when Frost stepped in.

She moved forward in a slithery, silky way totally at odds with her brown suit. Kaitlyn saw her smile at the two men and take their hands.

God, not *now,* Kaitlyn thought. Flirting won't stop them. But this passed in a flash, because Frost was talking, and not in a sexy way, but bright and cheerful.

"You must be—Jim and Chris," she said, hanging on to their hands like somebody at a tea party. "My uncle told me about you. You're in the corporate group, right?"

The two men looked at her, then at each other.

"We're just looking around. I'm thinking of coming here in a few years, and these are my friends. My uncle said it would be all right, and he gave me his security pass."

"Your uncle?" one of the men said, not as sharp as before, but bewildered.

"Mr. Morshower. He's a senior partner—but you know him, because he knows you. Why don't you call him at home and check it out? He'll tell you everything's okay."

"Oh, Sam," one of the young men said weakly. Funny that Kaitlyn had suddenly realized they were young. "I mean, Mr. Morshower." He threw a look at the other young man and said, "We won't bother him."

"No, no. I insist," Frost said. "Please call him." She actually picked up a phone from one of the secretaries' desks.

"That's all right," said the second young man. He looked unhappy. For the first time Kaitlyn was able to look at them as people. One had brown hair and one had black hair, but they were both wearing white shirts and striped ties knotted all the way up, even at this hour, and they both looked pale and somewhat harassed.

"Are you sure?" Frost asked, sounding disappointed. She put the phone back. The young men gave wry, watery smiles.

"Can you find your way out?" they asked, and Frost said of course, they could. Kaitlyn hardly dared to say anything, but she managed to smile at them as she walked past, and back down the hall, and toward the elevators.

Her chest was squeezed again, but this time the pressure was from inside. She was so bursting with laughter that she could hardly contain it until they were in the elevator.

Then they were all laughing, howling, shrieking, almost falling down. Renny did fall down, drumming his heels on the elevator floor. They were insane. Kaitlyn very nearly kissed Frost.

"But how did you know?" she said. "Did Joyce tell you?"

"No, no." Frost tossed her ash blond head impatiently. "I got it from them. I could've done it just from a piece of their clothing or one of those stupid fat silver pens they had in their pockets."

"Those were Montblanc pens. And they weren't silver, they were platinum," Gabriel said quietly, and then they all had to be quiet because they'd reached the lobby. Frost swerved toward the red-coated guard to sign out, but Gabriel pushed her past him and into the street. The guard looked after them, came to the door.

"Step on it," Kait said to Gabriel as they scrambled into Joyce's car.

"It's called psychometry," Frost said to Kait after another period of hilarity. Gabriel was driving wildly through the streets of San Francisco.

Kaitlyn had heard of psychometry. You could tell a person's whole history by handling a personal object. "But why did you pick Mr. Morshower?"

"Because I could tell they were afraid of him. They were supposed to have something—a merger agreement?—sent to his client by the FedEx deadline today and they haven't done it."

Frost reeled the words off glibly, but Kaitlyn could tell she wasn't really interested anymore. And the resourcefulness and sanity that seemed to have taken her over during the crisis was fading. The inner fogginess was coming back. It was as if intelligence were a tool this girl used, and then threw away when it wasn't needed anymore.

That put a damper on Kaitlyn's excitement. The feeling of having brilliantly outwitted a cruel world was dying away. For a while it had made her breathless, but now . . .

We really are crooks, she thought with a mental sigh.

And she was afraid of Frost's powers. Anybody who could find out that much about you with a touch was dangerous. Frost had already touched Kait when they were in the backseat of Joyce's car. Had she found anything out?

Must not have, Kaitlyn concluded, or Joyce wouldn't have sent me. Maybe it helps that I've developed shields in the web. But I'll have to be careful—one false step and . . .

"Just try not to get a ticket," she said to Gabriel, who was rounding a corner wildly.

He didn't answer. Great. He wasn't speaking to her again.

"Did I pass?" Kait asked Joyce.

Joyce looked at her, going through all the signs of being startled.

"What do you mean?"

"It was a test, wasn't it? So, did I pass or fail? I didn't do much."

They were sitting up in Joyce's room, drinking herbal tea in the wee hours of the morning. Renny and Frost had gone upstairs to drink something stronger, and Gabriel had gone with them, never glancing at Kait.

"Yes, it was a test," Joyce said at last. "The money will come in handy, but mostly I had to make sure that you were really one of us. Now you're a full member of the team—and if you ever think of crossing us, remember that you've participated in a felony. The police take a dim view of that."

She took a sip of tea and mused briefly. "You and Gabriel passed," she added. "As for Frost and Renny . . ."

"They did most of the work."

"But from what you've said, they also did a lot of stupid things." For a moment Kait thought Joyce was going to go on, to confide in her. But then Joyce stood up and said shortly, "We'll stick to other kinds of jobs from now on. Long distance, maybe. Mac is good at that."

"Is he?" Kait asked innocently. "What's his power? I don't know what he or Bri do."

She held her breath, sure Joyce wouldn't tell her. But Joyce shrugged and said, "His specialty is astral projection, actually."

Let your mind do the walking, Kait thought. It was Lewis's phrase. So Mac was responsible for the astral projections and psychic attacks against them on the way to Canada. "But we saw at least four figures," she blurted before she thought. "And one of them was Bri—I *recognized* her."

Joyce was setting the clock radio by the bedside and answered impatiently and almost absently. "Mac used to guide them, help them get away and then help them get back into their bodies. But anybody can do astral projection if they have the power of the crys—" She broke off so quickly her little white teeth actually snapped shut. Then she said, "Bed, Kaitlyn. It's way past time."

I knew they used the crystal to project themselves, Kait thought. I saw it beside their astral forms. But she didn't tell Joyce. She said, "Okay, but are you going to tell me what Bri does?"

"No. I'm going to go to bed."

And that was all Kaitlyn could get out of her.

Upstairs, Kaitlyn could hear the voices in Gabriel's room. Gabriel and Frost and Renny? Gabriel and Frost? There was no way to find out.

"Too bad I can't do astral projection," she muttered.

Lydia was asleep, of course, so there was no chance to talk to her. And no way to try out the secret panel downstairs—it was directly across from Joyce's room.

Nothing to do, then, but go to sleep . . . but it took her a long time to relax, and when she did, she had nightmares.

The next morning she saw Frost coming out of Gabriel's room.

Gabriel came out a moment later, while Kaitlyn was still standing motionless by the stairs. He was shrugging into his T-shirt. He looked particularly handsome in a just-roused, early morning way. His hair was very wavy, as if someone had run fingers through it to release the curl, his eyes were hooded and lazy and there was a faint smile of satisfaction on his lips.

Kaitlyn discovered that she wanted to kill him. The image that came to her mind was of hitting him with a rolling pin, but not in an amusing, comic-book sort of way. In a way that would make splinters of bone fly and splatter the walls with blood.

His expression changed very slightly when he saw her standing there. His eyes narrowed and his mouth soured. But he held her gaze stonily and walked by her without speaking.

"Today you'll do some testing," Joyce said to Kaitlyn after breakfast.

But before starting with Kait, Joyce settled the other psychics in. Testing had changed since the old days, Kaitlyn thought. Then, Joyce's experiments had been scientific, the kind of thing you could report in a journal article. Now, everything seemed oriented toward crime.

Jackal Mac, wearing swim trunks full of holes, was led toward the back lab with the isolation tank, and Kait heard Joyce saying, "Just take a look inside that safe in the city, see if the papers are there. Then try the long-distance job, check out that furnace."

Astral projection for felons, Kait thought. Is that how they knew the twenty million was in that filing cabinet? But how did they know to look in a filing cabinet in the first place?

Renny was practicing his PK, but not on a random event generator as Lewis had done. He had a collection of locks in front of him, as well as diagrams that looked like the insides of locks. Without touching anything, he was making the locks open and close.

Aha, Kait thought. Well, that makes sense. He needs to know what part of the lock to push with his mind to open it. PK doesn't give you magical knowledge about locks, just the power to poke around inside them.

It explained Gabriel's comment about Lewis not being able to open the combination lock on the crystal—wherever the crystal *was*. Kaitlyn would bet her last dime that Mr. Z had some sort of fiendishly complicated locking device, something that Lewis couldn't get a diagram for. Which meant the only way to open the lock would be to somehow figure out the eight numbers in the combination.

Whoa, girl. Take it easy. You've got to *find* that crystal first.

As soon as she'd thought it, Kaitlyn shifted nervously. Gabriel and Frost were sitting across the room by the stereo. But *he* was studying a pile of CDs and *she* couldn't tell anything unless she touched a person. Besides, she seemed to be studying Gabriel. She was looking more sleazy than grungy today, in an orange top cut so low that you could ski down the bare skin in front. Her hair had returned to its usual uncombed state and her lips were vivid tangerine.

"What are you doing?" Kait asked Bri, as a diversion.

Bri glanced up. "Can't you tell?"

She was holding a plumb bob on its line above a map. The plumb bob and line looked just like what Kaitlyn's father had used to determine if a surface was vertical, just a small weight hanging freely from a cord. The map was upside down to Kaitlyn and she could only make out "—Charlotte Islands."

"I'm dowsing," Bri said. She gave a boyish grin at Kait's surprise.

"I thought you used a forked stick for dowsing."

"No, stupid. That's for dowsing for water or gold or something. This kind is to find things that are far away, and you can do it for *anything.*"

"Oh." As Kaitlyn watched, the plumb bob began to swing in circles over a section of the map.

"See? All you got to do is think of what you're looking for. Sasha used to do the other kind of dowsing, only he didn't use a stick. He used coat hangers shaped like *l*s."

"Sasha?"

"Oh, yeah. You never met him." Bri snorted laughter. "He was blond and pretty cute, critty pute. Cute."

"Was he one of Mr. Z's first students?" Kaitlyn asked quickly. "Part of the pilot study, like you?" Bri seemed to be on the verge of one of those bizarre attacks which always ended in her repeating nonsense words until it drove everyone crazy.

"Yeah, him and Parté King. Not his real name. Parté King was a bike messenger in the city, a real skinny guy. Both terrific psychics."

"But what happened to them? Are they dead?"

"Huh? They—" Suddenly Bri's face turned cold, as if someone had turned off a light switch inside her. She looked up at Kait and her face was hard. "Yeah, they're dead," she said. "Sasha and Parté King. You wanna make something of it?"

Joyce was coming out of the back lab. Kaitlyn moved away from Bri's carrel feeling depressed.

The dark psychics were nicer to her now, sure, but it was like a geyser pool bubbling between eruptions. Ready to go off in her face at any minute.

The doorbell rang.

"That's the volunteers—would you get them, Gabriel?" Joyce said bustling around with her clipboard. "Frost, I'm going to have you do some psychometry with them; Kait, I'm going to start you with some remote viewing."

She sat Kaitlyn in a carrel with a photograph in front of her. It was an eight-by-ten glossy of a wall safe.

"I want you to concentrate on the picture and draw anything that comes into your mind," she said. "Try to imagine what might be *in* the safe, okay?"

"Okay," Kaitlyn said, concealing a surge of rebellion. This was *not* legitimate research, and she was losing her taste for larceny.

"I'm going to put this on your forehead," Joyce added, producing a piece of masking tape.

This time the surge was one of alarm, and Kait couldn't hide it. "An electrode over my third eye?" she asked as lightly as she could.

"You know what it is. Since you haven't been

exposed to the big crystal, we'll use this to enhance your powers."

"Well, why don't you expose me to the big crystal, then?" Kait asked recklessly. "Those little chips give me a headache, and—"

"Sorry, that's up to Mr. Zetes, and he doesn't want you anywhere near it. Now, hold still." Joyce's tone said she'd had enough. Her eyes had gone as hard as gems and she barely pushed aside Kaitlyn's bangs before slapping the tape on Kait's forehead.

Kait felt the piece of crystal cold against her skin. It was bigger than the piece Joyce had used in the old days, maybe because now Joyce wasn't trying to conceal it. This one felt the size of a quarter.

Knowing where it came from, she could scarcely keep herself from tearing the tape off. But then she saw Gabriel in the doorway, looking sardonic and amused.

You don't have anything against the crystal, do you? After all, you're one of us. . . .

Kaitlyn shot back, *I'm not one of* them. *But I guess you are.*

Right, angel. I'm one of them—and don't you forget it.

Kaitlyn left the tape alone.

But she didn't want to help Joyce with the safe. She stared at the photograph, then shut her eyes and just scribbled, taking the time to think.

She understood now how the dark psychics had attacked them on the road to Canada. First Bri probably dowsed to figure out where they were. Then Jackal Mac guided their astral forms to the right location. After that, they could assault their victims with weird apparitions or with Renny's long-distance

PK. Simple. You could terrorize people without ever going near them.

And now Joyce was expecting her to join in the long-distance crime wave, to help them visualize some safe to break into.

Wait a minute.

If she could see into a safe, why not a room? Why not try to visualize the secret room below the stairway?

Without opening her eyes, Kait groped for a new piece of paper. She'd never tried to visualize a specific place before, but the remote viewing process was old hat by now. Stretch out and let your thoughts drift. Block out any external noises. Let the darkness take you down. . . .

And now, think of the secret room. Think of walking up to the door, visualize that hallway lit by fluorescent greenish light. Walk up to the door . . . and let the darkness take you. . . .

Her hand began to cramp and itch.

Then it was dancing and skidding over the paper, moving of its own accord while Kaitlyn floated in darkness. Sketching fluidly, easily. Kaitlyn held her breath and tried not to be anxious, tried not to think or feel anything.

Okay, slowing down—is it done yet? Can I look?

She couldn't resist the temptation. One eye opened, then both were open and wide. Chills swept over her, as she stared, not at the piece of paper her hand was still working on, but at the first one, the one that was supposed to be only scribbles.

Oh, God, what *is* it? What have I done?

10

It wasn't her usual style. It was cartoonish, but *gruesome* cartoonish, like the new breed of comic books. At first Kait thought it might be a picture of her beating Gabriel to death with a rolling pin.

But those long tear-shaped things flying out at the edges were flames. Flames, fire. It was a fireball or an explosion, circular, with smoke billowing every which way, and the shock waves moving outward like ripples on a pond.

And in the center was a stick figure of a person. Like Itchy the cat after Scratchy hits him with a flame-thrower. Arms waving, legs splayed in a grotesque dance.

Ha, ha.

Except that since Kait's drawings always came true, somebody was going to get burned. Somebody involved with that safe, maybe? Kait tried to recapture what she'd been thinking about while scribbling. Too much. Psychic attacks, Canada, Bri dowsing, Jackal

Mac on the astral plane, Renny's PK. And the safe, of course, even though she'd tried not to think about it.

This picture could involve any of those things. Kait had a very bad feeling about it, made worse by a nagging, growing headache.

What about the other picture? The one that was supposed to be visualizing the secret room? Kait looked at it and wanted to slam her fist on the table.

Garbage! Trash! Not literally, but the drawing was useless. It wasn't the inside of a room at all, and it certainly didn't show a crystal. It was a line drawing of a sailing ship on a pretty, wavy ocean. Sitting on the deck, right below the sails, was a Christmas tree. A nice little Christmas tree with garland and a star on top.

Kaitlyn's eyes were stinging with pain and fury. The first picture left her helpless. The second was useless.

And that makes *me* completely hopeless.

Suddenly she couldn't hold her feelings in. She crumpled them up with a savage motion and threw them as hard as she could at Frost. One hit Frost on the cheek, the other hit Frost's volunteer.

"Kaitlyn!" Joyce shouted. Frost leaped up, one hand to her cheek. Then she made a rush for Kait, her nails clawed.

"Frost!" Joyce shouted.

Kaitlyn put a foot out to block Frost. In elementary school she'd been a pretty good fighter, and right now it felt good to fend Frost off. And if Frost whacked her, she was going to whack right back. She felt calm and queenly standing there ready to kick Frost in the chest.

"Come on, snowflake," she said. "Come get me!"

"I will, you!" Frost shrieked, charging again.

"Gabriel, help me! Renny, you stay in that seat!" Joyce shouted.

Joyce and Gabriel dragged Frost back and sat her down hard in a chair. Kait was tempted to go after her, but didn't.

"Now," Joyce said in a voice to cut through steel, "what is going on?"

"I got mad," Kaitlyn said, not at all sorry. "Everything I draw is *trash.*"

"Smash," Bri said quietly. Kait had an urge to snicker.

Joyce was staring at Kait, lips compressed, brow furrowed. Abruptly, she pulled the tape off Kait's forehead.

"How do you feel?" she said.

"Bad. I have a headache."

"Right," Joyce muttered. "All right, you go upstairs and lie down. But first you pick up those papers and put them in the trash can where they belong."

Stiff-backed, Kait stalked over to the crumpled wads, picked them up. Then, as Joyce turned back to her clipboard, she faked throwing them at Frost again. Frost went red, and Kait hurried out of the room.

Upstairs, she shut the door of her bedroom and wondered what had come over her.

Was she crazy? No, of course—it was the crystal. Joyce had used a big piece of the crystal and it had made Kaitlyn act like the psycho psychics.

And I must be pretty crazy to start with, because it didn't take much, Kaitlyn thought. Maybe Bri and the others were a lot saner than me to begin with. I wish I could have seen them before . . .

She let out her breath, trying to make sense of her feelings. She'd really been furious there, furious and completely indifferent to any consequences her actions might have. She'd would happily have scratched Frost's eyes out.

Well, maybe that wasn't so crazy. After all . . .

Kaitlyn sat on the bed heavily. She kept trying to tell herself she didn't care about Gabriel—but if she didn't care, why did she hate Frost so much today?

And Gabriel certainly didn't jump up to defend me, she thought. He probably enjoyed watching us fight.

Kait rubbed her throbbing forehead, wishing she could go outside and lie under a tree. She needed air. Idly, she toyed with the balls of paper in her other hand.

Then she looked up as the door opened.

"Can I come in? My riding lesson was canceled this morning," Lydia said. She sounded depressed.

"It's your room," Kaitlyn said.

She kept rolling the paper balls around, squashing them against each other. She'd taken them so Frost wouldn't pick them out of the trash can and laugh at them—but was that the only reason? Now she wondered if it hadn't also been some survival instinct kicking in.

None of her drawings was really worthless. Maybe she'd better keep them.

"What's the matter?" Lydia asked.

Kait frowned. Lydia was picking *now* to talk? "I've got a headache," she said shortly, and dropped the paper balls in a drawer.

Then she remembered her promise to Lewis. She glanced at Lydia out of the side of her eye.

The smaller girl looked very neat in a brown riding habit. Her heavy dark hair was pulled away from her small pale face, and her green eyes showed up more than ever. Neat and rich—and miserable.

"Have you got a boyfriend?" Kait asked abruptly.

"Huh? No." She hesitated, then added, "I'm not after Gabriel, if that's what you mean."

"It isn't." Kait didn't want to talk about Gabriel. "I was thinking about Lewis—did you ever notice him?"

Lydia looked startled—almost frightened. "Lewis! You mean Lewis Chao?"

"No, I mean Lewis and Clark. Of course Lewis Chao. What do you think of him?"

"Well . . . he was nice to me. Even when the rest of you weren't."

"Well, he thinks you're nice, too. And I told him—" Kaitlyn caught herself. Oh, Lord, this headache was making her stupid. She'd almost said that she'd told Lewis *yesterday* she'd bring him up. Frantically, she tried to think of another way to end the sentence.

"I told him that you'd think you were too good for him. That you'd just laugh at him. That was a long time ago," Kaitlyn finished at random.

Lydia's eyes seemed to turn a darker green. "I wouldn't laugh. I like nice guys," she said. "I don't think *you're* very nice. You're turning out just like them," she added, and left the room, slamming the door.

Kaitlyn leaned back against the headboard, convinced she just wasn't cut out to be a spy.

And she still didn't feel quite herself. One thing was certain, she couldn't let Joyce put her in contact with the crystal again. It made her lose control, and when she lost control anything could happen.

And another thing was certain, too. She couldn't use her power to visualize the hidden room downstairs, and Joyce wasn't going to let her anywhere near it. So the only solution was for her to go down there herself.

But *when?*

Still rubbing her forehead, Kaitlyn toed her sneakers off and lay down.

At first she shut her eyes just to ease the headache. But soon her thoughts began to unwind and her muscles relaxed. This time there were no nightmares.

When she woke she had that feeling of desertion again. The house seemed too quiet, the warm air too still.

At least her headache was gone. Moving slowly, she got off the bed and tiptoed to the door.

Silence.

Oh, they *wouldn't* leave me alone again. Not unless it's a trap. If it's a trap, I'm not going anywhere.

But she had a *right* to go downstairs. She lived here; she was a full member of the team. She could be going down to get a diet soda or an apple.

Down the stairs, then.

And she had a right to look around downstairs. She could be looking for the others; she could be lonely. She kept the right words on her lips.

"Joyce, I just wanted to ask you—"

But Joyce wasn't in her room.

"Are you guys still testing—?"

But the front lab was empty. So was the back lab.

And the kitchen, and the dining room, and the living room. Kaitlyn pushed aside the living room curtains to look outside the house. Nobody playing hacki sack or Frisbee tag. Only juniper hedges and acacia trees. She couldn't even see Joyce's car.

Okay, so maybe it's a trap. But it's too good an opportunity to miss.

Heart beating in her throat, Kaitlyn crept toward the paneled hallway under the staircase.

The middle panel, she thought, with one guilty

glance behind her at the French doors leading to Joyce's room. She ran her fingers over the smooth dark wood, reaching up to find the crack that was the top of the door.

Okay, she was in front of it. Now to find the place Lewis had showed her. She shut her eyes and concentrated on the images she'd gotten from Lewis. They weren't exactly visual, more like just a feeling of how she should move her hands. He'd found something around this level—and then he'd pushed with his mind. She would push with her fingers.

And then he'd moved over *this* way, and down, and pushed again. Kaitlyn pushed again, pressing hard.

Something clicked.

Kaitlyn's eyes flew open. I did it! I actually did it!

Excitement bubbled up from her toes, fizzling out to fill every part of her body. She was *impressed* with herself.

The middle panel had disappeared, sliding to the left. Stairs led downward, illuminated only by faint reddish lights at foot-level.

The bubbles seemed to be making a fizzing in her ears now, but Kaitlyn tried to listen over it. Still, silence.

Okay. Going down.

With each step into the red dimness, she felt a little of the effervescence leaving her. This wasn't a nice place. If she'd been a few years younger, it would have made her think of trolls.

At the bottom she groped for the light switch she knew should be there—and then snatched her fingers back. Too much light wasn't good. If there was somebody in the room at the end of the hall, they might notice.

But if she didn't turn on the light, she'd have to

walk the whole way in darkness. Just the thought made her knees unsteady.

There was no help for it. Tensing her muscles, she put a hand on the wall to guide her and began walking forward. In a moment she had to put the other hand out to feel for obstacles. She was blind.

Each step was hard, and she had to clench her teeth tighter and tighter to make herself keep going. The red staircase behind her began to feel more and more tempting.

Oh, God, what if somebody came and saw the panel open and closed it *and locked her in here?*

The thought was so terrible that she almost turned around and ran. Instead, she used the energy to force herself forward. And *one* more step, and *one* more step—

Her outstretched fingers encountered a door.

Her need for light was so great that she reached automatically for the knob, without listening to see what might be on the other side. But instead of a knob, her fingers found something like a calculator built into the door.

What was it? She could feel little square bumps in a regular pattern. It really did feel like a calculator.

Oh, you idiot. You *idiot.* You must still be stupid from the testing this morning. It's a combination lock. Not one of those padlock kinds; one of the fancy ones, where you punch numbers on a keypad.

And if this was the combination lock, then behind that door . . .

It was *in* there. That grotesque thing with the obscene crystalline growths all over it. It was squatting in there just a few feet away.

Kaitlyn was swamped by a feeling of evil.

And then—she heard noises.

From behind the door.

They were in there with it.

Oh, God, I'm so stupid, I'm so stupid. Of course, they're in there. This is where they go in the afternoons, they go to the crystal, and they're all sitting in there around it *right now.*

Don't panic, don't panic, she told herself, but it was too late. She *was* panicking. She hadn't even asked Lewis how to shut the secret panel. She was incompetent and stupid and they were right inside there and she didn't have time to get away.

Another noise sounded—very close to the door.

Suddenly Kaitlyn was moving, without thinking, without caring where she was going. With great stocking-footed leaps she was sailing down the hallway toward the red stairs. She reached the first step and began to scramble up, banging her knee, ignoring it, scrambling on. Using her hands. She got to the top of the stairs and the white light of the hallway blazed into her eyes. That light was the only thing that stopped her, kept her from running through the living room and out of the house—or up to her bedroom to hide under the bed. She was almost like an animal in her blind instinct to get under cover.

"Kaitlyn, what on *earth—?*"

The voice was high and light, surprised. Kaitlyn turned terrified eyes on Lydia.

"What happened? Did they do something to you?" Lydia was looking past her down the stairs.

A tiny bit of Kaitlyn's mind returned. There was a chance, just a chance for help—for salvation. Lydia knew about the panel; Lydia seemed worried about Kaitlyn.

"Oh, Lydia," she said, and her voice came out a croak. "I—I . . ."

She'd meant to lie, to say that she'd been down with the others and she'd gotten scared. But somehow what came out was, "Oh, Lydia, I know I shouldn't have gone down there. But Joyce never lets me do anything. I just wanted to see—and now Joyce is going to be *furious*. I don't know how to get the panel shut."

Lydia was looking at her with level green eyes.

"I just want to do the things they do," Kaitlyn said, then blurted, "I'm sorry if I was mean to you before."

There was a pause. Kaitlyn's heart was beating so hard she was dizzy. Lydia was staring down at the staircase, lower lip caught between her teeth.

Finally she looked up. "So you want to do the things they do. You're one of them. Okay." She leaned forward and touched the left wall quickly, in three different places.

The panel slid shut, concealing the gaping hole.

Kaitlyn stood, not knowing what to do. Lydia stared at the floor.

"Be careful, Kaitlyn," Lydia said, and then she hurried away before Kaitlyn could recover.

Kaitlyn stood under the spray of hot water, trying to get warm. Her legs were still wobbly and she was developing a magnificent bruise on one knee.

Lydia knew.

There was no doubt in Kaitlyn's mind. The one in the house who wasn't psychic was the one who'd found her out. Kaitlyn's lies hadn't fooled her for a minute.

So why had she helped Kaitlyn?

Oh, it didn't matter. Just please let her not tell Joyce. Kaitlyn flexed her cold hands under the flood of water.

But there was no way to ensure that. The only way

to keep safe was to leave. And Kaitlyn couldn't do that. No matter how frightened she was, she couldn't leave when she'd come so far. If she could just stick it out until Monday—and if she could get Rob to give her the shard—

—and if she could figure out the combination.

She had to, to get into that room alone.

Drying herself as she went, Kaitlyn headed for her art kit.

Last time she hadn't been concentrating on the right thing. She'd been trying to see inside the room—and heaven only knew why she'd gotten the garbage she had. Maybe Joyce kept a Christmas tree in with the crystal. Maybe there was a ship in a bottle in there. Anyway, now she knew what to think about.

Numbers. She needed numbers for that combination lock. And with her own art materials, with her beloved pastels and her faithful sketchbook, she was going to get those numbers.

Door shut tight, ceiling light off. Kaitlyn threw a T-shirt over the lamp on the nightstand to dim it. Okay, that was the proper ambiance. Hair swathed in a towel, feet tucked under her, she put pastel to paper.

She had never worked so hard at blanking her mind. She *threw* herself down the chute into the waiting darkness. The itch and cramp took over her fingers and she felt them moving, reaching out to snatch new pastel sticks, swirling colors across the page.

A few minutes later she looked at what she'd done.

I can't believe it. I can't *believe* it!

It was another ship with a Christmas tree.

This time in color. The ship's sails were dove white, the planks were tinted sienna brown, the pretty curly waves were three shades of blue. And standing proud·

ly on the deck was a celadon green Christmas tree with poppy red garland and a yellow ocher star.

Kaitlyn wadded the paper up in a fury and threw it at the mirror.

She wanted to break things. She wanted to throw something heavier—

The door burst open.

Instantly, Kaitlyn's fury disappeared and terror rushed in to fill the vacuum. Lydia had told them. They had all run up here to get her. She could hear thudding footsteps in the hall behind the figure in her doorway.

"Hey, Kait, how come it's so dark in here?" Bri shouted. Without waiting for an answer, she added, "Come on! Get dressed!"

For what, execution? Kait wondered. She heard her own voice saying almost quietly, "Why?"

"Because we're celebrating! We're all going out to the club! Come on, get dressed, put your best duds on. Plenty of *guys,*" Bri added slyly. "You got something to wear? I could lend you something."

"Uh—that's okay, I've got something," Kaitlyn said hastily. She could just imagine what sort of "duds" Bri might have to lend. But Bri's urgency was contagious, and Kaitlyn felt herself being propelled toward the closet. "I've got a black dress—but why are we celebrating?"

"We did a job this afternoon," Bri said, shaking her clasped hands over her head like a boxer. "An astral job, a real big job. We killed LeShan."

"I met her on the stairs. She said she had to see you," Tony's friend said. Rob, Lewis, and Anna were sitting in the tiny one-room apartment. Rob peered behind Tony's friend at the person who had to see them.

"I've been tracking you from house to house," the girl said. She had clusters of curly yellow hair and the profile of a Grecian maiden. Despite the yellow hair, her complexion was olive and her eyes almond-shaped like Lewis's. She was very pretty.

And familiar. "I know you," Rob said. "You were— you were with the Fellowship."

"Tamsin," Anna said, before the girl could.

The girl—Tamsin—nodded at her. She looked as if she were trying to smile, but it didn't work. The smile turned into a trembling of her lips, then her head went down and she started to cry.

From the doorway, Tony's friend said, "I'll catch you guys later," and left hurriedly.

"What is it?" Rob was trying to lead the girl to a chair. His initial excitement at seeing her had deflated like a pricked balloon. He'd thought the Fellowship had sent someone to help.

"I came to help," the girl choked out, as if she could hear his thought—and probably she could. The Fellowship were all psychics. "LeShan sent me."

"Then what's the matter?" Anna asked quietly, putting a gentle hand on Tamsin's quivering shoulder.

"Nothing was the matter—until a little while ago. Then I felt it. I felt him die. LeShan is dead."

Rob's skin tingled with shock. He had to swallow hard. "Are you sure?"

"I *felt* it. We thought we'd be safe from them on our new island. But they must have found him. I felt him die."

She's really upset, Lewis said silently.

She was, Rob thought. Not just upset but helpless— the way the people of the Fellowship tended to be when they didn't have a leader. He didn't send the thought to Lewis because he had the feeling Tamsin could hear.

"And now I don't know what to do," Tamsin said, almost wailing it. "LeShan was going to tell me when I got here. I came all this way and I can't help you at all."

Rob looked at Anna, as if he might find something comforting to say in her face. Anna was so wise. But Anna's gaze, dark and liquid with tears, held his only a moment, then quickly dropped.

Angry with himself, Rob put an arm around Tamsin. He said, "Maybe Meren—"

"Mereniang is dead, too," Tamsin whispered. "She died on the way to the island. There's no help anywhere, no hope!"

11

Kaitlyn sat on Lydia's bed with the black dress on her lap. She had been reaching for it, glad that she'd brought it and that it had hung out with no wrinkles, when Bri had told her.

Now she just sat. She didn't need to ask Bri any questions. She knew the whole truth.

Queen Charlotte Islands. That's what the map had said. In Canada. That must have been where the Fellowship had gone when they'd left Vancouver Island. Bri had dowsed for them with that map.

And Jackal Mac had checked the furnace out. Some furnace where the Fellowship were living. Kaitlyn knew because she had a picture of it—a picture of a fireball, of a furnace exploding. And a man in the middle of it.

All of them had gathered around the crystal this evening and sent out their astral forms. They'd left their bodies and gone to the Queen Charlotte Islands and then Renny had used his PK.

Oh, LeShan. Kaitlyn twisted the chiffon of the black dress between brutal fingers. I liked you. I really liked you. You were arrogant and angry and impatient and I really, really liked you. You were *alive*.

Caramel-colored skin. Slanting lynx eyes. Softly curling hair that seemed to have an inner luminescence, pale and shimmering brown. And a spirit that burned like midnight fire.

Dead.

And now Kaitlyn had to go and celebrate. No way to get out of it. They would know if she tried to make some excuse. If she was going to be one of them, she had to hate the Fellowship as they did.

Feeling very brittle, very light, and unstable, Kait went over to the mirror. She pulled off the towel and her clothes and put on the black dress. She began to mechanically run her fingers through her wet hair, when she suddenly realized something.

I look like a witch.

In the dim light, with her long hair falling about her shoulders, drying just enough to be a halo of red, with the black dress and her bare feet and the pallor of her face . . .

I do. I look extremely witchy. Like somebody who might go walking down the street like this, barefoot, hair wild in the breeze, singing strange songs, and all the people peeping out at me from behind their curtains.

The fitted spandex bodice *did* make her look slim as a statue, and the sheer chiffon skirt swirled from hip to midcalf. But it wasn't vanity that held her there looking. It was a new sense of her own competence, of determination.

Anybody who looks this witchy *must* be able to call

down a curse. And that's what I'm going to do. Somehow, I'll make them all pay, LeShan. I'll avenge your death. I promise.

I promise.

People were calling outside. Lydia was opening the door apologetically.

"I just heard," she said. She looked as hangdog and slinking as Kaitlyn had ever seen her, but also bitterly satisfied, as if she'd been proved right. "I told you my father would win. He always does. You were smart to come in on this side, Kait."

"Could I borrow a pair of nylons?" Kaitlyn asked.

Mr. Z was in the living room when they all came downstairs. Kaitlyn supposed he'd been in the hidden room with them, directing the work. He gave Kaitlyn a courtly nod as she walked toward him in a pair of shoes borrowed from Frost.

He looked amiable, but Kaitlyn could *feel* his savage joy. He knew she was hurting and he liked that.

"Have a good time, Kaitlyn," he said.

Kaitlyn lifted her head, refusing to give him the satisfaction.

Gabriel was there, too, handsome in dark clothes. Kaitlyn turned appraising eyes on him. He didn't look disturbed over LeShan's death—but then he had no reason to like the Fellowship. Their philosophy said they couldn't open their doors to anyone who'd taken a human life . . . no matter what the circumstances. Because Gabriel had killed by accident and in self-defense, they refused to let him in. So now Gabriel wasn't upset.

Everyone else was delirious with happiness.

Mr. Z saw them off, and they took two cars. Kait rode in Lydia's car with Bri and Renny. Joyce took

Gabriel, Frost, and Jackal Mac. Kait spent the drive plotting how to make them all pay—Gabriel, too.

The club was called Dark Carnival. Kaitlyn stopped musing on revenge to stare. It was like nothing she'd ever seen before.

There was a line of people waiting to get in the door. People wearing *everything*. Unimaginable outfits. They looked bizarre and more than a little scary.

Traffic stopped the car for a while near the door and Kaitlyn was able to watch what was going on. A doorkeeper with a lip-ring and a Liverpool accent was saying who could get in immediately, who should wait, and who should just go home. Those who got in: a guy with purple glittery lipstick and silver aluminum curlicues for hair. A girl in an evening gown of black spiderweb. A chic Italian-looking girl in a white unitard and black velvet shorts—very short.

"He keeps out people who aren't cool enough," Bri said in Kaitlyn's ear, leaning heavily on her back. "You have to be either famous or completely beautiful or—"

Or dressed like a cross between a Busby Berkeley show and something from a science fiction movie, Kaitlyn thought.

"So how are we going to get in?" she asked quietly.

She was watching the losers—the people who couldn't get in. The normal people who weren't exciting or weird enough, waiting outside behind cords, sometimes crying.

"We've got invitations," Lydia said in a dead voice. "My father has connections."

She was right. The doorkeeper let them right in.

Inside there were strobe lights, super black lights, and colored lights, all flashing in an atmosphere so full of smoke Kaitlyn could hardly see anything but the flashing rainbow.

The music was loud, a throbbing beat that people had to shout over. On the dance floor a girl with long shiny hair was kicking high over her head.

"Isn't it great?" Bri yelled.

Kaitlyn didn't know what it was. Loud. Weird. Exciting, if you were in the mood to celebrate, but surreal if you weren't.

I'm going to avenge you, LeShan. I promise.

She glimpsed Joyce walking toward the dance floor. Jackal Mac, the lights reflecting on his head, was giving an order to a scantily clad cocktail waitress.

Where was Gabriel?

Bri had disappeared. Kait was surrounded by people with wings, people dressed in cellophane, people with spikes for fingernails. Everywhere she looked were falls of Day-Glo hair. Enormous false eyelashes. Slanted eyebrows, silver-glittering eyebrows. No eyebrows. Pierced bodies.

If she hadn't been so cold with anger over LeShan, Kaitlyn might have been scared. But just now nothing could touch her. A man in a leopard-skin unitard and a mask beckoned her to dance and she followed him to the floor. She didn't really know much about dancing, except what she'd done at home, watching the TV and dreaming.

It was too loud to talk, and she didn't really care what the leopard-man thought of her—so it was the perfect opportunity to muse on revenge again.

And that was how she solved the mystery of the combination lock.

It wasn't like in books, where the faithful sidekick makes some offhand remark and then the famous detective sees all. There was no particular reason why it came to her. But every minute or so her mind would go back to her problem.

I need to get to that crystal. Which means I need to get the combination.

And once when her mind went back to it, she thought, "But maybe I already have the combination. One drawing was a real prophecy. What about the other?"

And then the other thought was simply *there,* full-blown, a question asking itself in her mind: How can a Christmas tree and a ship be eight numbers?

Well, *Christmas* had a number, of course. A date. December the twenty-fifth, 12/25. Or 25/12 if you were thinking the twenty-fifth of December.

The dark room rocked under Kaitlyn's feet. The leopard-skin man was walking away, but she didn't care. She backed up to a railing, her eyes on the flashing lights.

She was trembling with excitement, her mind racing to follow this new idea to the end, like a spark running down a line of powder.

The ship. The ship is another number. And what number? It could be the number of masts or the number of crew or the number of voyages it made. Or a date, a date when the ship sailed—but what kind of ship is it?

A window opened in her stomach and she felt hollow with dismay. She didn't know anything about ships. How long would it take to research, to speculate?

No, stop. Don't panic. The picture was drawn by your unconscious, so it can't be much smarter than you are. It couldn't take a date and make it into a ship if you didn't *know* the date and ship already.

But I'm so stupid, Kaitlyn argued back. Rotten in

history. I only know the simplest dates—like "In fourteen hundred ninety-two . . ."

Columbus sailed the ocean blue.

That sparkly, curly blue ocean. Three colors of blue. Drawn with an excess of care.

She'd found the answer.

Kaitlyn knew it, she felt certain. But a nagging murmur of dissent was starting in her brain. Mr. Z wouldn't make the combination that simple. He wouldn't begin it—or end it—with 1492. Anyone *glancing* at it would remember. Someone breaking in might try it at random.

That was when Kaitlyn had her second brainstorm. Supposing the combination didn't begin or end with 1492—not all together. The Christmas tree had been in the middle of the ship, so supposing the combination was 14/12/25/92. Or 14/25/12/92.

Good heavens, or even 1/12/25/492. Or . . .

Kaitlyn cut her busy brain off. I'll think of all the possibilities later. But I'll try the easy ones first. And I'll—

A guy with a bald head was darting a black-stained tongue at her. Kaitlyn recoiled, then realized it was Jackal Mac.

"What's the matter? Scared of me?"

Kaitlyn stared into the jackal eyes. "No," she said flatly.

"Then come dance."

No, Kaitlyn thought. But she was a spy and her most important job was to not get caught until she got the shard to the crystal. Nothing else was important.

"Okay," she said, and they danced.

She didn't like the way he moved in on her. Not like slow dancing, he wasn't trying to hold her, but he kept moving toward her, forcing her to back up. Otherwise his swinging arms and gyrating hips would have made contact.

She saw Frost and Gabriel together on the floor. Frost fit right in here; she was wearing a silver baby doll dress and silver ankle boots. She kept brushing against Gabriel's body as she danced.

Well, at least she wasn't as exposed as that woman wearing a negligee. Or that man painted orange who seemed to be wearing almost *nothing*.

"Hey, baby! Pay attention!"

Jackal Mac was closing in again. Kaitlyn stepped back and collided with a woman in space-age neon sunglasses.

"Sorry," she muttered, inaudibly over the music. She edged away, heading for a deserted space below the bandstand. "Look, Mac, I'm kind of tired—"

"Sit down and rest."

He was backing her farther into the space, below and slightly behind the stage. Kaitlyn tripped over a cord or cable. She couldn't keep walking backward like this.

"I think I just want something to drink. Would you like something?"

It was strange that her voice was so calm. Because suddenly she was very scared.

They were in an isolated little nook here, where the music was loudest. No one from the dance floor could really see them. Certainly no one could hear them. It was smoky and dark and humid and it felt like a trap.

"Yeah, I'm kinda thirsty," Jackal Mac said, but he was blocking the way out. His eyes gleamed in the dimness. He had one hand up, resting on the stage, and suddenly Kaitlyn got a whiff of his sweat.

Danger.

It was like red warning lights flashing in her head,

like the sound of sirens. She could *feel* his mind, cluttered and trashed and nasty as his bedroom. Nasty as the red-haired man had been.

"I'm thirsty, you know, but not for a drink. Gabriel told me how you used to take care of him."

Not like the red-haired man after all. Jackal Mac had a different aberration. He didn't want to hurt her body, he wanted to suck her brain out.

You bastard, Kaitlyn thought with white-hot fury, but she didn't mean Jackal Mac. Her hatred was for Gabriel.

He'd told this—animal—about what Kait had done for him. The most private moments she'd ever had with anyone. Kaitlyn felt as if she'd been violated already, ripped open for everyone to see.

"What else did Gabriel tell you?" she said in a voice that was hard and distant and unafraid.

Jackal Mac was surprised. His head bobbed, ape-like, then his black-stained tongue came out to lick his lips.

"He said you were always chasing him. I guess you like it, huh?" Sliding his arm down to shoulder level, he moved closer. "So you gonna make this easy, or what?"

Kaitlyn held her ground. "You're not a telepath. I don't know what you think—"

"Who says you need to be a telepath?" Mac laughed. "This is about energy, pretty girl. We all need energy. Everybody who's a friend of the crystal."

The crystal. Of course. Mr. Z's way of keeping them all in line. It had made them all psychic vampires like Gabriel. And it satisfied them all, provided them with energy . . . unless you were like Jackal Mac and wanted something extra.

He wants me to be afraid, Kait thought. He enjoys

that, and he'll like draining my energy best if I'm fighting and screaming. That little extra kick.

I hate you, Gabriel. I *hate* you.

But it didn't prevent her from saying what needed to be said.

"And you think Gabriel's going to like it if you mess around with me?" she asked. "He didn't like you messing with his room."

Mac's eyes took on an almost injured expression.

"I wouldn't touch Gabriel's woman," he said. "But that's Frost now. He was the one who said I should check you out."

His teeth shone white in the darkness.

For an instant, Kaitlyn felt only numb. Gabriel had thrown her to Jackal Mac like a bone. How could she *live* with that?

And then survival instinct took over and she realized that she wouldn't have to live with it if she didn't do something fast.

Jackal Mac was reaching for her with his blunt, restless hands. She knew the routine. There were several transfer points, but third eye to third eye or lips to spine were best. She would bet that Mac wanted her spine.

So *relax.* Relax and let him get behind you. No, pretend you're going to cooperate.

A part of her mind was yammering at her, insisting that there was a way to yell for help. A vocal scream would be lost in the throbbing music, but she could scream mentally. Gabriel had come the last time; he might come if he thought Mac was killing her.

But I *won't* scream, she thought, cold washing over her like an icy waterfall. I won't scream even if he does kill me. I wouldn't take Gabriel's help if I knew it would save my life.

Gabriel had set this human beast on her. Let Gabriel live with the consequences. Besides, he might hear her screams and just smile.

"Come on," Kaitlyn said to Mac, aware she hardly sounded seductive. "I don't mind. Just let me get my hair out of the way."

His hands with their ugly, chewed-up nails hovered in the air. She stepped toward him, but to one side, grasping her hair with one hand, pulling it off her neck, watching his eyes follow her movements greedily.

"Okay and just let me do—*this.*" While his eyes were on her bare shoulders, she slammed a heel into his shin. He made a thick, startled sound of surprise and pain, more like a pig than a jackal. He lunged toward her—

—but she had kicked the loose cord between his feet. He stumbled, tangled in it. Kaitlyn didn't wait to see if he recovered his balance or not. She was running.

She reached the dance floor, plunged into the crowd. Fell into someone's arms. A poetic-looking young man wearing a shirt with a large collar and flowing white sleeves.

"Hey—"

Kaitlyn reeled away. Where was Joyce? Nobody else could keep Mac from following her out here, from dragging her back. . . .

There. Joyce and Lydia. Kaitlyn wove unsteadily toward them through the crowd.

"Joyce—"

She didn't get any farther. A roar was beginning behind her. Jackal Mac was parting the crowd like Moses parting the Red Sea. But unlike Moses, he was doing it with fists and elbows, and the Red Sea was getting mad.

"You don't need to explain," Joyce said tightly to Kaitlyn.

As Kaitlyn watched, Mac ran into a short woman with lacquered hair. He shoved her aside. A large man wearing chains lunged forward to grab him.

"Here comes Renny," Lydia said.

Renny appeared with a bottle. Kait couldn't tell if he was attacking Mac or defending him, but suddenly glasses were flying, people were throwing punches. Jackal Mac picked up a chair and lifted it over his head.

Screams split through the music. Hefty men in suits were running in from all directions.

"You girls get out of here," Joyce said. Kaitlyn could feel that she was angry and exasperated almost to tears. Here she was, out to celebrate in her pink St. John dress with the rhinestones, and Mac was ruining everything. If Kaitlyn hadn't known why Joyce was celebrating, she might have felt sorry for her.

As it was, she took Lydia's arm and propelled her toward the Exit sign. Lydia waited until they were in the car to speak.

"What happened?"

Kait shook her head, then leaned her temple against the cool window. Everything inside her was sick and sore. Not from Mac's attack. From knowing Gabriel had egged him on. And from the hole in the universe where LeShan had been.

It's a filthy world, she thought slowly. But I'm going to do my part to clean it up. And then I'll never have to look at Gabriel again. I'll go as far away from here as I can go.

It was very late when she heard Joyce bring the others home that night. There was a lot of thudding on the stairs, a lot of banging and laughing and cursing.

"They scare me," Lydia said softly from the other bed. "The way they are. What they can do."

They scared Kaitlyn, too. She wanted to say something comforting about how things were going to change, but she didn't dare. Lydia wasn't evil, but she was weak—and besides, no one was to be trusted. *No one.*

"Think about something else," Kaitlyn said. "Did you ever find a cow alarm clock around here?"

"No. A what?"

"An alarm clock shaped like a cow. It was Lewis's. It used to go off every morning, this sound like a cowbell and then a voice shouting 'Wake up! Don't sleep your life away!' And then it would moo."

Lydia giggled faintly. "I wish I'd seen that. It sounds—like Lewis."

"Actually, it sounded like a cow." Kaitlyn could hear Lydia snorting softly in the darkness for a while, then silence. She pulled the covers over her head and went to sleep.

The next day she was confronted with a problem. Everyone else was exhausted and lethargic, so Joyce had canceled all testing. She had the day to herself—but she couldn't figure out how to get in touch with Rob.

Call the Diaz house? Not from inside the Institute. Much too risky. And she had no excuse for walking off alone to find a pay phone. She didn't want to do anything that might look suspicious.

But she *needed* to talk to Rob, to tell him to bring the shard on Monday. She didn't want to waste any more time.

She was sitting at the desk in her room, tapping a pencil and wondering if she dared ask to borrow Lydia's car, when a noise at the window made her turn around.

A kitten. A big kitten, almost a cat. It was pawing at the screen.

Kaitlyn almost smiled despite her mood. You funny baby, how did you get all the way up here? she wondered, and went to open the screen. The kitten butted its head against her and rasped her knuckle with a tongue like a furled pink leaf until Kait rubbed the black velveteen fur between its ears.

What a funny collar. Way too thick. That must hurt you. . . .

It was a piece of paper, wrapped around and around the blue nylon stretch collar and secured with masking tape.

A note.

Suddenly Kaitlyn's heart was beating hard. She looked down into the backyard below the window. Nobody in sight. Then she glanced over her shoulder, toward the closed door of the bedroom.

Eyes on the door, she pulled at the tape with her fingernails, tearing the note free.

12

The man at the airport and the lady with the pitchfork are dead. The water's too hot. Meet me at the old rendezvous soon and the dish will run away with the spoon. Pick your time, just let me know. Send a message in a bottle.

The note was neither addressed nor signed—Rob had thought it less risky that way, Kaitlyn supposed. But she understood what it said.

Mereniang was dead, too. LeShan was the man who'd accosted her at the airport, and the first time they'd seen Meren she'd been pitching cow dung. Rob thought Kaitlyn was in too much danger now, and he wanted her to come to the gym, where he'd whisk her away from the Institute permanently. She was supposed to pick a time when she could get away and send a note back.

Kaitlyn sat for a moment, rolling the pencil between her fingers. Then she straightened her shoulders, tore a sheet out of her sketchbook and began to write in a heavy, determined hand.

> The hotter the water, the better witches like it.
> No date today. Same time, same place tomorrow.
> Bring the magic knife. I've done my homework
> and know my numbers.

She hoped Rob would remember Tony saying "I see you got the magic knife for Marisol." And he hoped he would understand that she *couldn't* leave now; she knew where the crystal was kept and she knew the combination to get to it.

The kitten was nudging her, rolling, asking for pets. Kaitlyn stroked it, then wrapped the note around its collar and taped it securely. She opened the screen and held her breath.

Out went the kitten, without a backward glance. Anna must have implanted the suggestions very well.

Now, Kaitlyn thought, leaning back. Nothing to do but wait for tomorrow at noon. And hope Rob keeps his date.

"I can't let you do it alone," Rob said.

"But don't you *see?* It's the only possible way."

"No," Rob said flatly.

It was noon on Monday. They were hiding in the gym itself, which seemed safer than the entrance.

Kaitlyn looked at Lewis and Anna for help, but they were both looking pretty helpless. As if they couldn't figure things out. Rob was the one who'd made up his mind.

"I can't let you take it back to the Institute by yourself. I'm going with you—I'll sneak in whenever you do."

He just wasn't thinking it through. "But what if we get caught sneaking into the house?"

"What if *you* get caught with the crystal? That would be just as bad as being seen with me."

"No, it *wouldn't*," Kaitlyn said, straining to keep her voice patient. "I can hide the crystal—or at least there's a chance that I could hide it quick if I heard somebody coming. But I can't hide *you*. What am I going to do, stick you under a sofa pillow?"

Rob was trying to be patient, too—she could see and feel it. And he was losing the battle. "It's . . . just . . . too . . . dangerous," he said with slow emphasis. "Do you really think I'm going to sit around, safe in somebody's apartment, while you take all the risk? What does that make me?"

"Smart. Rob, I'm hoping I can get to the crystal today, but that may not be possible. Joyce could have the lab door open; somebody could be sitting in the living room where they can see the secret panel. I may have to wait around for days and watch for my chance. *You* can't sit that long in the house with me—or even outside," she added, cutting him off. "Gabriel would feel you there, just like he did before. And then it would be all over; he's really our enemy now."

She had thought this through, and she didn't intend to budge. And she could see Rob knew it. His expression suddenly changed; his jaw set, his mouth straightened into a grim line. A golden blaze sparked in his eyes. He looked, Kaitlyn thought, like a good guy pushed too far.

Without a word, he reached for her, grabbed her around the waist. Kaitlyn felt herself lifted, her feet leaving the wooden gym floor.

"I'm sorry, but I've had enough," he said. "You're coming back to the car."

A few days ago, Kaitlyn might have thought this funny. But now . . .

Put me down!

The volume of it shocked Rob into loosening his grip. The sheer fury in her eyes kept his mouth shut as Kaitlyn pulled away from him.

Anna and Lewis were shocked, too—and frightened. Kaitlyn knew they could feel the anger pouring off her like invisible waves. She stood like a queen, feeling tall and terrible and when she spoke each word came out like a white-hot chip of steel.

"I am *not* an object, something to be picked up or carried away or passed around. *Gabriel* thought that's what I was. He was wrong. You're both wrong," she said to Rob.

His hair was tousled, making her suddenly think of a little boy. His eyes were dark amber and wide. There was utter silence in the gym.

"*I* am the only one who can decide what will happen to me," Kaitlyn went on very quietly. "No one else. *Me.* And I've already made my decision. I'm going back to that place and I'm going to try to stop them any way I can. Whether you give me the shard or not is *your* decision, but I'm going back anyway."

She had never spoken to him like this before, and she could see that he was confounded. Stricken. Kaitlyn tried to make her voice gentler, but she could hear the steel underneath it.

"Rob, don't you see, this thing is bigger than just us. You're the one who taught me that things can be bigger than people. You made me *want* to make a difference. And now I have a chance to do it. Timon died and LeShan died and Mereniang died, and if somebody doesn't stop the Institute more people are going to die. I *have* to try and stop that."

Rob was nodding slowly. He swallowed and said, "I understand. But if something happened to you—"

"If something terrible happens to me, then at least I know that *I* chose it. I went because I decided to go. But *you* don't have anything to do with it. . . . Do you understand?"

Anna was crying. Lewis was almost crying.

And Rob—seemed shocked into submission. He looked at Anna as if that were somehow his final appeal.

Anna blinked away tears. Her face was compassionate, sad—and still. Too deep a stillness to be simply resignation.

"Kait's right," she said. "She'll go if she says she'll go. You can't say for her. Nobody can ever say for somebody else."

Then Rob looked back at Kait, slowly, and she knew that he was seeing her as an equal for the first time. An equal not just in brains or psychic power or resourcefulness, but in every way, with exactly as much right to risk her life as he had to risk his.

Equal and *separate*. It was as if at that moment they split apart, became two independent creatures. If Rob had ever had a fault in their relationship, it was thinking he had to protect her. And Kaitlyn had encouraged it in a way, by thinking that she needed to be protected. Now, all at once, they were both realizing it wasn't true.

And once Kait knew that, she realized that in the last few minutes she had grown in his eyes. Rob respected her more, even loved her more than ever before . . . in a different way.

But he was still having a hard time grasping that he was *really* going to have to stand here and watch her walk away and take the risk herself. So he gave it one last try, not with force, but with entreaty.

"You know, I've been wondering if we should maybe wait just a little to use the shard, anyway. It did cure Marisol, you know. You didn't see that, Kait, but it was wonderful. And there are a lot of other people in that hospital. I was kind of hoping . . ." He shrugged, his face wistful.

Kaitlyn was moved. But before she could speak, Anna did. Anna's face was even more compassionate than before, more sad—and more certain.

"No, Rob," she said quietly. "That's the one thing we *can't* do. It doesn't belong to us; it's just on loan. Timon gave it to us for destroying the crystal. We *can't* just go around using that much power that isn't really ours. Something bad would come of it."

Then she put a gentle hand on Rob's shoulder. "You've got power of your own that you can use to help people—and that should be enough. You'll have your chance, Rob."

Rob stared at her for a long moment, then nodded. He looked from her to Kaitlyn, and through the web, Kaitlyn got just a glimpse of his thought. He was awed and a little confused at being caught between these two farsighted women. She could feel him wondering how they'd gotten so wise while he'd stayed dumb.

And thinking there was nothing for him to do but agree.

"So it's settled," Kaitlyn said quietly. "I'll take the shard and go back to the Institute, and you'll go back to Tony's friend's apartment."

"We left Tamsin there," Anna said. "We'll tell her what you're doing. She'll be rooting for you, Kait, and so will Marisol."

Kaitlyn was glad to talk about something ordinary, because she had the feeling that any minute she might start crying. "Marisol's really that much better?"

"She's still in the hospital because her muscles are weak and she has to learn to use them again. But Tony says it'll only be a few days before she's walking. Oh, Kait, I wish you could have seen his face when he came to see us! And his mom and dad—they called and just thanked us over and over. We couldn't get them off the phone."

"And Tony said he was going to light a candle for you," Lewis put in. "You know, in church. Because Rob told him you were in danger."

Kaitlyn's throat was swollen and her eyes kept filling with warmth. She gulped. "I'd better take it and get going."

Rob knelt and opened the duffel bag he'd brought. He took out the crystal shard, opened Kaitlyn's backpack, and put it in. Kaitlyn knew that he was doing it himself as a sort of symbolic offering, an admission that she was right. She also knew that he had to fight to make every move.

He stood up, very pale, and held the backpack out to her.

"Call us when it's over," he said. "Or if you think you can't do it before tomorrow. And, Kait?"

"Yes?"

"If you don't call us by tomorrow, I'm coming in. That's not negotiable, Kaitlyn; that's *my* choice. If I don't hear from you, I'm assuming that something's gone wrong, and all bets are off."

What could Kaitlyn say?

Good luck, Lewis said silently as she hugged him. *I'll be thinking about you.*

Be careful, Anna said. *Be as clever as Raven and get yourself out safe.* She added a few words in Suquamish, and Kaitlyn didn't need a translation. It was a blessing.

Last of all, she hugged Rob. His eyes were still sore from the hard lesson he'd just learned. He held on to her very tightly. *Please come back to me. I'll be waiting.*

How many times had women said that to their men who were going off to war?

The swelling in Kaitlyn's throat was getting bigger by the minute. *I love you all,* she told them. Then she turned around and walked toward the back door of the gym, feeling their eyes on her. She knew they stood in perfect silence as she went out onto the blacktop, and then onto the baseball field, watching and watching until she was out of sight.

Kaitlyn was heading straight back for the Institute. It was only about a mile. She'd told Rob that she might have to wait for days to get to the crystal, but she knew that her best chance was right now. Bri, Renny, and Lydia were at school—and Gabriel was supposed to be. That left Frost and Jackal Mac in the house with Joyce.

I should be able to get in without them noticing, she thought. And then maybe they'll all go into the back lab or something, and I can get to the panel.

The walk was actually pleasant. Kaitlyn found herself noticing the sky, which was a beautiful blue with just the right amount of wispy clouds. The sun was warm on her shoulders, and the hedges by the sidewalk were dotted with starlike yellow flowers. It's spring, she thought.

Strange how you enjoyed the world more when you

thought there was a chance you might be leaving it soon.

Even the Institute looked exotic and beautiful, like a giant grape monument.

Now came the hard part. She had to sneak in so as not to get caught, but do it without *looking* sneaky. So that if she *were* caught, she could say she'd come home from school sick.

After some thought, she let herself in the kitchen door. The kitchen was right by the front lab, but no one in the lab could see her until she passed the lab doorway.

Music was coming from the lab. Good, that should cover any sounds. Squaring her shoulders, Kait walked boldly by the lab doorway, forcing herself to glance inside casually, forcing herself not to tiptoe.

That one glance showed her Frost sorting through a tray full of watches and keys, while Joyce sat beside her with a notebook. Frost was facing the back lab—great. Joyce was facing Frost, but bent over her notebook. Pretty good.

Jackal Mac was nowhere in sight. Kait prayed he was in the back lab, in the tank.

Still forcing herself *not* to be stealthy, not to creep, she walked through the dining room and out and around the staircase. She looked around the corner and saw the little hallway that led to the other door of the lab.

Okay, how to make this look casual? I've got to wait here . . . maybe I'm tying my shoe.

Without taking her eyes off the figures in the lab, she knelt and undid her shoelace. Then she stayed that way, with the laces in her hands, watching Joyce.

I can't go into the hall until she turns around or goes into the back lab. It takes a few seconds to get the panel to slide back, she could just glance up and see me from where she is now.

Time dragged by. The backpack began to feel heavy, dragging at Kaitlyn's shoulders.

Come on, Joyce. Move. Go get a book from the case or something. Go change the CD. Do anything, just *move*.

Joyce stayed put. After what seemed like an hour, Kaitlyn decided that she was going to have to risk stepping out anyway—and then she saw Joyce was getting up.

Kait's vision seemed to go double. Joyce's face was a tan blur. Then Joyce's back was a pink blur. Joyce was going into the back lab.

Oh, thank you! Thank you!

The instant the last bit of pink disappeared, Kaitlyn stepped into the hall. No time to be stealthy, no point in looking casual. All that mattered was to be *quick*.

Her fingers stabbed out at the wood paneling, once and then again. The click seemed agonizingly loud. She threw a glance at Frost—Frost still had her back turned.

The panel had recessed. Kaitlyn stepped into the gaping hole.

Down the stairs. Quick. Quick.

She'd never learned the secret of closing the panel from inside. Well, it didn't matter much. As long as she got to the crystal. She didn't care if they discovered her after that.

As she reached the bottom stair she shrugged off her backpack and pulled out a flashlight. She'd taken it from the kitchen drawer that morning.

Quick. Move quick. The little circle of light showed her the way.

Aha. There it is.

The combination lock shone softly on the wall by the door, looking like something from a science fiction set. A door to the starship *Enterprise*.

Although her heart was beating in all sorts of funny places—her throat, her ears, her fingertips—Kaitlyn felt calm. She'd rehearsed this all in her mind last night.

Put the backpack down. Flashlight in your teeth. Take out the paper with the possible combinations on it. Make every move count.

Paper in one hand, she began to punch in numbers with the other.

Each little rubber pad gave under her fingertips, and the number she'd punched appeared on an LED display at the top.

1 ... 4 ... 1 ... 2 ... 2 ... 5 ... 9 ... 2. Enter.

Nothing. The LED display blanked out.

Okay. *Next!*

1 ... 4 ... 2 ... 5 ... 1 ... 2 ... 9 ... 2.

Again, nothing. Tiny threads of panic began to unwind in Kaitlyn's gut. Okay, so she still had six combinations to go, but she'd used the best two. What if Mr. Z had changed the numbers? She should have drawn again last night to make sure. Oh, God, she hadn't even *thought* of that. . . .

Wait a minute. I didn't press Enter.

She pressed it. Immediately she heard a sort of pleasant hum, an accepting sound that reminded her of an ATM machine getting to work.

With a soft click, the door opened away from her.

I did it! It worked! Oh, thank you, Columbus—I'll love you forever!

Her heart was beating all over now, her entire skin tingling with the pulses. Excitement and fear swam inside her, and she had to take a deep breath to keep her head.

Okay, quick, now, *quick*. A light might be seen upstairs, so get the shard out first.

She fumbled getting it out of the backpack. The flashlight kept sliding out from under her chin. The paper with the combinations had fallen on the floor. She ignored it.

Okay. *Got it.*

With both hands, she held the crystal shard.

It had never felt so good to her. Cold and heavy and sharp, it was like a weapon in her hand, strengthening her. It seemed to be telling her, *Don't worry about anything from here on in. All you have to do is get me to the crystal. I'll take care of things from there.*

Yes, Kaitlyn thought. Now.

In the end, it had almost been too easy. Why had Rob been so worried about her?

Standing tall, holding the crystal like a spear, she pushed the door open and stepped into the office. It was dark and she'd lost the flashlight. She reached for the wall, fingers groping across it. She found a light switch and got ready to throw it, planning to charge toward the great crystal as soon as she could see. A battle yell, some legacy of distant Irish ancestors, gathered in her throat.

Now . . .

She threw the switch—and froze.

The charge never happened. The crystal was there, all right, huge and deformed and grotesque as she remembered. But it wasn't alone. There were two—other things—in front of it.

Kaitlyn's eyes opened wide as she saw them. She felt her lips stretching open, not for a battle yell, but for a scream. A scream of perfect terror.

13

At first all Kaitlyn was able to take in was her feeling of disgust and horror. It was something like the disgust she'd felt at home when her dad would turn over a shovelful of earth in the garden—and reveal something soft and squirmy or hard and chitinous hiding underneath.

A little like that, but magnified hundreds and thousands of times.

She guessed these two things were human. Or had started out that way. But they looked so deformed and felt so *wrong,* they gave her the sick feeling she'd gotten when she first saw a potato bug, that huge, unnatural, semicrustacean-looking insect. Or when she'd seen her first picture by Hieronymus Bosch, the artist who did scenes from hell, with people who had lobsters' claws or windows in their bodies.

The other thing she knew immediately was that they were guard dogs. Mr. Z's new guard dogs, put here to protect the crystal.

Sasha and Parté King.

She knew them from Bri's descriptions—although it took a lot of imagination. Sasha had skin that was chalky white, unnaturally white, like something that had never seen the sun. Almost translucent, with lines of blue veins showing through. His eyes were like the red eyes of albino mice, or the blind eyes of cave fish.

He did have blond hair, as Bri had said. Hair that was not just unkempt but *full of things*. Bits of garbage and paper like the rubbish that covered the floor.

He looked like a slug: white, flaccid, immobile.

Then there was Parté King—whatever that weird name might mean. Bri had said he was skinny. Now he was skeletally thin, wasted away like someone about to die. Skin stretched across his bones—almost as if he had an exoskeleton, like a bug. His brown hair was falling out in clumps, exposing naked skull.

He looked like some kind of cricket, as if he would rattle if you shook him.

And they were both alive, even though they looked like nothing that could survive long. Kaitlyn realized with a qualm of pure horror that they *lived* down here, alone and insane, chained to the floor. Biting at people's ankles, grinning face-splitting grins.

She thought she was going to vomit.

"Muh-muh-muh," Sasha said, beaming. His teeth were wet; wetness spilled onto his chin. He made a wormlike movement toward her.

I should run, Kaitlyn thought dispassionately. Her thought seemed to die somewhere before it got to her legs. She stood still and watched the swollen white grub thing inching across the floor toward her. It was like a human being in the process of mutating into something. A pupa.

They weren't going to let her get to the crystal. She could feel the power of their minds like a curtain across the room. So strong it almost knocked her over, invading all her senses. The touch of their minds made her think of rotting things, bugs, pus.

Parté King was making a clicking noise in his throat. Pushing himself into a sitting position. They both wore canvas jackets which held their arms behind their backs with many straps.

Straitjackets.

Below that they wore garbage bags. Kaitlyn couldn't make sense of that until she realized: diapers.

Run, you stupid girl. Please run now.

Parté King fell over backward, his stick legs waving slowly in the air.

"Ch-ch-ch-ch-ch." He was still grinning.

So this is what happens to Mr. Z's old students. It could happen to you, too. A little too much time near the crystal and . . .

Hey, but they're still terrific psychics!

Please, *run*.

At last she seemed to tune in to her brain's terrified whimpering pleas. She turned around to run. She saw the open door of the office, took a wavering step toward it.

And ran into a sort of invisible wall, a thickening of the air. Cold air. Or maybe there was nothing wrong with the air, and it was just her muscles.

She couldn't move a step closer to the door. They had her; they were draining her volition, her will to run. She couldn't get away, and maybe she'd known that all the time.

Sasha laughed bubbles, like a baby.

"You poor things," Kaitlyn whispered. Pitying

them didn't change an ounce of her loathing for them. She knew somehow that they were beyond any kind of healing. Hurt worse than Marisol in her coma.

Even if they would let her approach them with the crystal shard, even if she were a healer like Rob, it wouldn't help. Kaitlyn *knew*.

Her knees were giving out. She let it happen, sitting on the floor and watching the creatures who shared it with her crawl closer. There was nothing to do.

Nothing except wait for Mr. Zetes to come.

"I thought you'd bring that to me," Mr. Zetes said. "Thank you, my dear."

He held his hand out for the shard. Kaitlyn looked at the long fingers with their square, perfectly manicured nails. She tried to stab him.

It was stupid. There were the human pupae behind her, dragging her every gesture into slow motion, and there were the psycho psychics behind Mr. Z. They'd all come to see the fun. Besides, Mr. Z himself was strong.

He took the shard from her, hurting her wrist. Deliberately, she thought.

"In a way, it's too bad you decided to come out of the closet now," Mr. Z said. "I wish you'd kept the pretense up for just a few more days. My next job for you was silencing the Diaz family."

His handsome old face was absolutely diabolical.

"I like your old students," Kaitlyn choked out. "The ones with very good minds. What a waste."

"Muh-muh-*muhhhh*," Sasha drooled behind her. "Muhhh."

Mr. Z glanced at him almost fondly. "They're still useful," he said. "The crystal has made them more powerful than ever; in a way, it's allowed them to achieve their true potential. I'm afraid you can't join them, though." He turned slightly, speaking over his shoulder.

"John, please put this in Joyce's room. Laurie and Sabrina, take Kaitlyn upstairs and get her ready. Paul, watch them."

Who are all those people? Kaitlyn thought whimsically. Jackal Mac took the shard and disappeared, presumably heading for Mr. Z's car. Frost and Bri stepped forward and each took her by an arm, leading her out of the office. Renny followed.

Joyce and Lydia were standing in the hallway by the hidden panel. Frost and Bri marched Kaitlyn by them.

As they reached the second floor, Kait spoke. "What's going to happen to me?"

"Never mind." Frost gave her a push and Kaitlyn stumbled into the room Frost and Bri shared. Frost's face was sparkling with malicious triumph. She looked almost beautiful, like a Christmas tree angel with hair made of spun glass. She had on bubble-gum pink lipstick, so glossy it reflected light.

"Bri? You going to tell me?"

Bri looked angry instead of triumphant. "You sneak. You dirty spy." Her deep boyish voice was rough with anger and revulsion. "You get what you deserve."

Renny stood just outside Bri's door, arms folded, his clean-cut narrow features severe. He looked like an executioner.

Frost was groping through a pile of clothes on the floor. "Here. Put this on."

It was a bathing suit, one piece, black-and-white striped.

Kaitlyn thought of saying "Why?"—but there

wasn't any point. She said, "I'm not going to undress in front of *him.*"

"Mr. Z told me to watch," Renny said. Not lecherously. Flatly.

"You got better things to worry about," Bri said, her voice harsh.

Kaitlyn decided not to argue. Bri was right; what difference did it make at this point? She turned her back to the door and stripped, ignoring Renny like a piece of furniture. She tried to hold her head high, make every movement regal and indifferent. Even so, by the time she had pulled the bathing suit on her face was burning, her eyes full of tears.

Frost tittered and snapped the elastic on Kaitlyn's back. But Bri said nothing and kept her head down. Even Renny seemed to avoid Kaitlyn's gaze as she turned around again.

"I'm ready."

They marched her downstairs.

Not back to the crystal room. Into the front lab. The door to the back lab was open.

And then Kaitlyn knew.

I will not scream, she told herself. I won't whimper and I won't scream. They'll just enjoy it more. They'd love me to start screaming.

But she was afraid she *would* scream. Or that she might even beg.

"Is everything ready?" Mr. Z asked Joyce. Joyce was standing in the doorway to the back lab. She nodded.

Jackal Mac was staring at Kaitlyn as if he wanted to drink her face through his eyes. His evil jackal eyes. His mouth was partly open, making her think of a panting dog.

Loving this. Loving it.

"You're going to end up like the ones downstairs," Kaitlyn told him. Jackal Mac grinned like a fox.

Mr. Zetes made a gesture, a formal gesture that reminded Kaitlyn of the first time she'd heard him speak. When he'd welcomed her and Rob and the others to the Institute, telling them how special they all were. It seemed like years ago.

"Now," Mr. Z said, addressing the whole group, "I think you all know the situation. We've discovered a spy. I'm afraid I suspected this from the beginning, but I decided to give her a chance." He looked at Joyce, who looked back with a blank face. "However, there's no longer any doubt about why she came to us. So I think the best solution is my original one."

He looked at each of the others in the room and spoke with genteel emphasis. "I want you all to witness this, because I want you to understand what happens when you break faith with me. Does anyone have any questions?"

The lab was silent. Dust motes hung in the slanting afternoon light. No one had a question.

"All right. John and Paul, take her in. Joyce will handle the equipment."

Fight, Kaitlyn thought. That was different than screaming. As Mac and Renny reached for her, she ducked sideways and tried to run, throwing a mule kick as she went.

But they were ready for her. Mac wasn't going to be faked out again. He simply tackled her as if she'd been a two-hundred-pound quarterback, knocking her to the floor. Kaitlyn saw stars and had a horrible sense of not enough air. She'd had the breath knocked out of her.

There was a confused time, and then she realized she was sitting up, being whacked on the back. She whooped in air. Then, before she could really get her bearings, she was being hauled to her feet.

Fighting was no good. She was helpless.

Then she heard a voice, thin, high, and frightened. To her astonishment, she realized it was Lydia.

"Please don't do it. Please don't—Father."

Lydia was standing in front of Mr. Z. Her pale hands were clenched together at waist level, not as if she were praying, but as if she were trying to hold her guts in.

"She can't fight you anymore, and you know it. You could just send her away. She'd never tell anyone about us; she'd just go away and be quiet and live. Wouldn't you, Kaitlyn?" Lydia turned huge green eyes on Kait. Her lips were white, but there was a fierceness in those eyes that Kaitlyn admired.

Good for you, Lydia, she thought. You finally stood up to him. You spoke out, even when nobody else would.

But someone else was speaking.

"Lydia has a point, Emmanuel," Joyce said in a low, carefully controlled voice. "I really don't know if we have to go this far. I'm not entirely comfortable with this."

Kaitlyn stared at her. Joyce's hair was sleek as seal fur, her tanned face was smooth. Yet Kaitlyn caught a sense of inner agitation almost as great as Lydia's.

Thank you, Joyce. I knew it couldn't all be an act. There's something good in you, deep down.

Kaitlyn glanced at the others.

Bri was shifting from foot to foot, scratching her blue-streaked head. Her face was flushed; she looked as if there were something she wanted to say. Renny was scowling, seeming angry but uncertain.

Only Jackal Mac and Frost still looked eager and

enthusiastic. Frost's eyes were shining with an almost romantic fervor, and Jackal Mac was licking his lips with his pierced tongue.

"Anyone else?" Mr. Z asked in a voice of terrible quiet. Then he turned on Joyce. "It's lucky for you that I know you aren't serious. You've managed to overcome your discomfort in much more squeamish situations than this. And you will now, of course—because you wouldn't want to join her in that tank. Or visit the room downstairs overnight."

A sort of shudder passed over Joyce's face. Her aquamarine eyes seemed to unfocus.

"And the same goes for the rest of you," Mr. Zetes said. "Including *you.*" He was looking at Lydia. He hadn't raised a fist; he hadn't even raised his voice. But Lydia flinched, and everyone else went still. His very presence cowed them all.

"Every one of you would go to jail for years if the police found out what you've been doing these last weeks," Mr. Zetes said, his face composed and satanic. "But the police will never have to deal with you. Because *I* will, if you cross me. Your old classmates downstairs will help. There is nowhere you can go to get away from us, nowhere you can hide that we can't find you. The power of the crystal can reach out across the globe and swat you like a fly."

Silence and stillness. The psychics watched the floor. Not even Frost was smirking now.

"Now," Mr. Z said in a grating whisper, "does anyone still have any objections?"

Some people shook their heads. Lydia, her shoulders hunched miserably, was one of them. Others just stayed still and quiet, as if hoping Mr. Z wouldn't look at them.

"Gabriel?" Mr. Zetes said.

Kaitlyn looked up in surprise. She hadn't realized Gabriel had arrived; she'd barely noticed his absence before.

He was frowning, looking like somebody who's arrived at a party to find it had started an hour earlier without him. "What's going on?" he said. He repeated it to Kaitlyn silently, his narrowed eyes on the black-and-white bathing suit. *What's going on? What did you do?*

"A disciplinary matter," Mr. Zetes said. "I hope there won't be any more like it in the future."

Kaitlyn didn't wait for him to finish, but spoke to Gabriel over his words. *None of your business. I despise you.* She threw the full weight of her contempt at him like someone throwing beer cans and rocks and bricks. And then, because Rob had taught her how to hurt him, she added, *Jailbird. You'd better do everything he says or he'll send for the police.*

She hadn't realized how much she hated him before this moment. All the loathing that she somehow hadn't felt toward Renny or even Jackal Mac and Frost, she felt for him. All the anger and betrayal. If she'd been closer, she would have tried to spit on him.

Gabriel's face hardened. She felt him pull away, felt the ice of his shields. He didn't say another word.

"All right," Mr. Z said. "You boys take her in; then we'll all go into the city for dinner. I think this calls for another celebration."

There was no point in fighting any longer. Mac and Renny dragged Kaitlyn into the back lab. She stood motionless in their grip while Joyce forced a mouth-piece into her mouth. It was connected to an air hose like a scuba diver's.

Now Joyce was pulling gloves over her hands and forcing her into a canvas jacket like the ones the creatures downstairs were wearing. Kaitlyn's arms were crossed, useless. Weights were being attached to a belt around her waist, and to her ankles.

She heard a voice behind her: Mr. Zetes. "Goodbye, my dear. Pleasant dreams."

And then Joyce was sticking something in her ears. Some kind of earplugs. Suddenly Kaitlyn was deaf.

They were pushing her forward.

The isolation tank still looked like a Dumpster. A lopsided Dumpster with a hurricane door. The door was open and they were forcing her inside.

She couldn't help it; she was going into this *thing*. This thing that they were going to close on her, that they were going to bury her in alive.

As the dark metal walls rose around her and the water came up to meet her, Kaitlyn's nerve broke. She did scream. Or at least, she tried. But the thing in her mouth muffled it like a gag and the earplugs dulled the rest of the sound. There was only silence as water enveloped her. And darkness.

She twisted, trying to get on her back, to see the door. To see the light for one last instant . . .

But all she saw was a rapidly diminishing rectangle of white. Then the metal door clanged shut. It was the last sound she was to hear.

Right from the beginning, it was very bad.

Remembering Bri's words ("Sure, it's cool. Cosmic, man!"), she had hoped that the tank might be pleasant at first. Or at least bearable. But it wasn't. It was a death trap, and from the first instant Kaitlyn felt a screaming inside her that wouldn't stop.

Maybe the difference was that she knew she was in here for good. They weren't going to let her out in an hour or a few hours or a day. They were going to keep her in here for as long as it took, until she was a *thing,* a drooling, vacant-eyed lump of flesh with no mind.

Her first thought was to try and beat the system. She would make her own noise; she would make herself feel. But even the loudest humming was dim and soon her throat grew sore. After a while she wasn't sure whether she was humming or not.

It was very difficult to kick with the weights on her legs, and when she did manage, she found the tank was lined with something like rubber inside. Between the drag of weights and water and the give of the rubber padding, she couldn't feel much of anything.

She couldn't pinch with her fingers, either; the gloves prevented that and dulled all sensation. Her arms were immobilized. She couldn't even chew her lips—the mouthpiece prevented it.

More, all these exertions tired her out. After trying everything she could think of, she was exhausted, unable to do anything but float inertly. The weights were gauged to keep her floating right in the middle of the water, away from the top and bottom of the tank, and the water temperature was gauged so that she had no sensation of hot or cold.

It was then that she began to realize the true horror of her situation.

It was dark. She couldn't *see.* She couldn't see *anything.*

And she couldn't hear. The silence was so deep, so profound, that she began to wonder if she really remembered what sound was.

In the endless dark silence, her body began to dissolve.

Once, when she'd just turned thirteen, she'd had a nightmare of a disembodied arm in her bed. She had half-woken one night to find that she'd been lying with her arms pressed together under her body, and that one of them had gone to sleep. She could feel it with her other hand: a cool, unnaturally limp arm. In her not-awake state, it seemed as if someone had put a severed dead arm in her bed. Her own arm was foreign to her.

After that, all her nightmares were of the cool blue arm snuggling up to her chin and then dragging her under the bed.

Now Kaitlyn felt as if *all* her limbs had gone to sleep. At first it seemed that her body had gone dead, and then she realized she didn't *have* a body anymore. At least, there was no way to prove she did.

If there were arms and legs in the tank, they weren't hers. They were dead, unholy, other peoples' limbs, floating around her, ready to kill her.

After a while, even the sense that there were other peoples' limbs around her faded. There was *nothing* around her.

She had no sense of being trapped inside the little Dumpster tank. She had no sense of being anywhere. She was alone in pure space, and around her was nowhere, nothingness, absence, emptiness.

The world had disappeared because she couldn't sense it. She'd never realized it before, but the world *was* her senses. She had never known anything but her internal map of it, made up from what she saw and heard. And now there was no sight, no sound, no map, no world. She couldn't keep hold of the conviction that there *was* a world outside—or that there was an outside.

Did the word *outside* have meaning? Could something be outside the universe?

Maybe there had never really been anything except her.

Could she really remember what the color "yellow" was? Or the feeling of "silk"?

No. It had all been a joke or a dream. Neither of those things existed. These ideas of "touch" or "taste" or "hearing"—she'd made them up to get away from the emptiness.

She had always been alone in the emptiness. Just her, just K—

Who was she? For an instant there, she'd almost had a name, but now it was gone. She was nameless.

She didn't exist either.

There was no person thinking this. No "I" to make words about it.

There was no . . . no . . . no . . .

A silent scream ripped outward. Then:

Kaitlyn!

14

Gabriel was frightened.

Frost sat beside him during dinner—Mr. Z's orders, he was certain. She touched him every other minute, stoking his wrist, patting his shoulder. Again, he felt certain, on Mr. Z's orders.

They wanted to know if he would try and reach Kaitlyn with his mind.

But the restaurant in San Francisco was too far from the Institute. Kaitlyn was long out of range, as Joyce must have told Mr. Z. Gabriel didn't even try to stretch out his mind; instead he worked on convincing everyone that he didn't want to. That he hated Kaitlyn as much as Jackal Mac did.

He must have done a good job, because Lydia was looking at him with burning green hatred in her eyes—when her father's head was turned, of course.

She wasn't the only one who looked unhappy. Bri had eaten almost none of her dinner. Renny kept swallowing as if he felt sick. And Joyce was holding herself rigid and expressionless, her aquamarine eyes fixed on the candle in the center of the table.

The club they went to next was also far away from San Carlos—but not quite as far. Frost left his side to dance with Mac. As soon as she was gone, Gabriel slipped the piece of crystal he had palmed out of his pocket.

It should increase his range—but enough? He wasn't sure. The only time he'd managed a telepathic link over such a long distance was when he'd been in agonizing pain.

He had to try.

With Mr. Z smoking a cigar and smiling benevolently at the dancers on the floor, Gabriel clutched the tiny chip of crystal and sent out his mind.

But the frightening thing was that even when he felt he'd stretched out far enough, he couldn't feel Kaitlyn. Her place in the web was filled with nothingness. Not even a wall, only blankness. Nobody nowhere.

Desperate, he kept calling her name.

There was a vision in her mind.

Whose mind? It didn't matter. Maybe there wasn't a mind at all, but only the vision.

A rose, full and blooming, with lush petals. The petals were a warm color that she had forgotten. At first it was a nice image, all those petals on one stem, separate but connected. It reminded her of something.

But then the vision went bad. The petals turned black, the color of the emptiness. The rose began to drip blood. It was hurt, mortally wounded. The petals began to fall . . . and on each there was a face, and the face was *screaming*. . . .

Kaitlyn! Kaitlyn, can you hear me?

Petals falling, dripping. Like tears.

Kaitlyn! Oh God, please answer me. Please, Kaitlyn. Kaitlyn!

There was desperation in the voice. Whose voice? And who was it talking to?

I couldn't contact you before. He had Frost sitting by me, touching me. She would have known. But now I have them convinced I don't want to talk to you—oh, please, Kaitlyn; answer. It's Gabriel.

Suddenly there was another vision. A hand dripping blood. Onto a floor. Gabriel's hand, cut by the crystal shard, dripping onto Marisol's floor.

And she had seen it, she, Kaitlyn. She was Kaitlyn. She had a self again.

Gabriel?

His voice came back, at a volume that hurt her. *Yes. Kaitlyn, talk to me.*

Gabriel, is it really you? I thought . . . you'd be mad. After I said . . .

She wasn't sure what she'd said. Or even what "saying" was.

Kaitlyn, don't be—don't even think about that. Are you all right?

It was a stupid question. Kaitlyn had no way to answer it in words, so she sent along the thin, quivering strand of the web that connected them a vision of what the emptiness was like. Nothingness, void, absence . . .

Stop. Please stop now. Oh God, Kait, what can I do?

Kaitlyn could feel the black well trying to suck her back into it; all she had to hold on to was the slender connection with Gabriel, like a tiny shaft of light in a dungeon. It was keeping her sane at the moment, but it wasn't enough. She needed more, she needed . . .

You need to see and hear, Gabriel said.

I don't even remember what those things are like, Kaitlyn told him. She could feel hysteria bubbling in her, stealing her rationality.

Gabriel said simply, *I'll show you.*

And then he began to give her things, with his mind. Things *he* had seen and heard, things from his memory. He gave her everything.

"Remember what the sun's like? It's hot and yellow and so bright you can't look at it. Like this. See?" In her sense-starved condition his voice seemed like a real voice not like telepathy. He was giving her the sound of talking. And sending her a picture. As soon as Kaitlyn saw it she remembered. The sun.

That's good, she said. *It feels good.*

"That's what it looks like in summer. I grew up in New York, and sometimes in the summer my mom would take me to this place by the ocean—remember the ocean?"

Blue-green coolness. Hot sand between the toes, gritty sand in the bathing trunks. Water foaming and hissing, children shrieking. The smell and taste of salt.

Kaitlyn drank it all in greedily, hungry for every nuance of sight or sound. *More, please. More.*

"We'd go up to the boardwalk, just her and me. She'd always buy me a hot dog and an ice cream. She didn't have much money, because the old man drank it all, but sometimes she'd make him give her a dollar to fix something he really liked for dinner. Then she'd get me the ice cream—remember ice cream?"

Creamy, blobby coldness. Stickiness on her chin. Rich, dark taste of chocolate.

I remember. Thank you, Gabriel.

He gave her more. All his best memories, everything he could think of that was good. Every golden afternoon, every skateboard ride, every moment with his mother when he was seven years old and sick with the fever that gave him his power.

Everything he was, he gave to her.

Kaitlyn devoured the sensations, filling herself with the reality of the world outside. She was drenched in sunshine and cool wind and the smell of burning leaves and the taste of Halloween candy. And music; she hadn't realized how Gabriel loved music. At fourteen, he'd wanted to play in a garage band. He was jamming with the drummer one night, trying to get more in sync—and then the drummer was lying on the floor, clutching his head. Pierced by Gabriel's mind. When Gabriel tried to help him up, he ran screaming.

A week later, Gabriel was on his way to the psychic research center in Durham, where his principal and his mother and the social worker hoped someone could teach him control. His father's last word to him had been: "Freak."

"Never mind about that," Gabriel said. He was giving her only good things, nothing depressing. She could feel that he didn't want her to see his father's stubbly face with the bleary red eyes. Or feel the burning hot shock of his father's belt.

It's all right, Kaitlyn said. *I mean, I won't look at anything you don't want me to, but you don't have to worry about me . . . and I won't ever tell anyone, and I'm so sorry. Oh, Gabriel, I'm so sorry. And . . .*

She wanted to tell him that she understood him now, in a way she'd never understood anyone before. Because she was *with* him. It wasn't even like being in the web; it was much closer than that, much deeper. He'd torn down all the barriers and put his soul into her hands.

I love you, she told him.

"I love you, Kaitlyn. From the very beginning."

She got a sense then, of how he saw her. Bits and pieces from his memories of her. Her eyes, smoky blue, with the strange dark rings in them, framed by heavy black lashes. Her skin tasting like peaches. Her hair crackling when she brushed it, flame-colored, silky but full of electricity.

She could sense, too, scraps of what he'd thought about her over the weeks. Lines from their lives together. *That kind of girl might be too interesting, might tempt you to get involved . . . A girl who challenged him, who could be his equal . . . Her mind was a place of blue pools and blazing meteors . . . She stood slim and proud as some medieval witch princess against the dawn.*

"And then I thought you'd betrayed me," he said. "But you really came to protect me, didn't you?"

With that, Kaitlyn realized that he'd seen as deeply into her mind as she'd seen into his. She had thought he was the one giving, while she had only received . . . but of course, he'd had to join with her completely in order to share his life with her.

He knew everything, now.

And then he came on something that sent shock waves through Kaitlyn.

"Jackal Mac said—*what?*"

Kaitlyn could feel the memory he was looking at. *He said you told him to check me out.*

Gabriel's cold anger filled the universe.

"I never said that. I never talked to him about you at all."

I know, Gabriel. She did know, she was certain.

"But Lydia knew how you gave me energy on the trip to Canada. She must have told him—"

177

Gabriel, forget about it. His fury was hurting her, filling her with images of death, of Jackal Mac spitting up bone splinters. *Please think me something nice.*

So he did. All that night, he thought her beautiful music and hillsides of wild mustard flowers and the smell of fresh pencil shavings and the taste of banana marshmallow candies. And the touch of his hands, the way he would do it if she ever got back in the world again.

Rob stared at the edges of the afghan that served Tony's friend for a window curtain. He didn't move, because he didn't want to disturb the others; Anna and Lewis and Tamsin on the floor. Even the black kitten Tony had given Anna was lying curled and still. But Rob couldn't sleep.

Light was showing around the blanket edges. Morning. And Kaitlyn hadn't called last night.

He had a very bad feeling.

There was no good reason for it. Kaitlyn had told them she might have to wait and watch her chance. That was probably what she was doing.

But Rob was empty and sick with fear.

Rob?

He turned to see Anna looking up at him. There was no sign of drowsiness in her face or her dark eyes.

I couldn't sleep, either. She put a hand on his arm and he put his hand over it. Just the feel of her warmth gave him some comfort.

You want to go and look for her now, don't you?

Rob turned from the window again. Her steady gaze, her calm face, and her gentle presence in the web all strengthened him.

"Yes," he whispered.

Then we'll go. I think we should, too. Let's wake up Lewis and Tamsin.

Kaitlyn knew it was morning because Gabriel said so.

"I think they're going to take you out soon. Mr. Zetes drove up a little while ago, and now Joyce is knocking on all the doors upstairs."

Another circus, huh? Kaitlyn asked. She didn't know how she felt about the outside world anymore, but the thought of everyone staring at her was definitely appalling.

"I'll be with you," Gabriel said.

As the night had gone on, she'd gotten more and more of an odd sense from him. A feeling that ran beneath the thoughts they were sharing, that he was keeping away from her. Although it was tightly controlled, she recognized it as pain.

Gabriel, are you all right? I feel—are you hurt, somehow?

"I have a sort of headache. It's no problem. Do you feel it now?"

Once again, she had the sense that he was concealing something. But concealing it better.

"Okay, Joyce is telling us to come downstairs." After a moment, he said, "We're in the lab."

Yeah, time for the unveiling. Kaitlyn laughed silently, nervously. *I wonder what they're going to think. I suppose I should act crazy.*

"I think it's your best chance. Kait—I don't know how I can save you right now. The others don't like what the old man is doing—I think Joyce asked him to take you out this soon—but they're afraid of him. And I can only fight one of them at a time."

Kaitlyn knew. Gabriel's destructive power operated most strongly when he could touch his victim, and it took time. He couldn't hold off Jackal Mac and Renny while killing Mr. Z, for instance.

And you're weak, she told him. *From helping me, I know. I'm sorry. But we'll manage somehow—maybe they'll just put me back in the tank.*

Then she realized something that made the blood start beating in her ears. *Gabriel, wait, wait! Rob is coming. I forgot.* She'd forgotten about the outside world. *All you need to do is wait until he gets here, then he can help.*

"It depends on what Mr. Z is going to do to you, whether we can wait. He's giving a speech now. On and on."

I don't want to hear it. Gabriel, you do know that Rob didn't mean the things he said at Marisol's house. He was mad at you. Hurt. And he felt betrayed. But that's because he really cares about you. You know that, don't you?

Even now, Gabriel refused to say it. But Kaitlyn had seen inside him too deeply to be fooled. Her question was rhetorical. Gabriel *did* know. His feelings for Rob were all mixed up with guilt and jealousy and resentment of Rob's effortless ability to do good and be good, and to go through life being loved. But Kaitlyn thought that Rob would be pleased with the feeling Gabriel had under that. He admired Rob. Respected him. Would have liked to be somebody Rob could like.

But he does like you, Kaitlyn said again, and then she realized they were opening the door of the tank.

The clang was a different sort of sound than Gabriel's mental voice, and she thought that if she had really been in silence all yesterday afternoon and night—maybe fifteen hours at a guess—she wouldn't have recognized what sound was anymore, and screamed in fear. She was spared having to fake that because they couldn't hear her.

Hands pulled at her, the touch as shriekingly dissonant as the door clang. Everything was so *harsh.* Her skin was so sensitized that even the gentlest pressure would have hurt, and these hands weren't gentle.

Then light struck her eyes. It both hurt and dazzled, confusing her. She couldn't really see anything, only the whiteness, with occasional shapes blocking it. Squinting helped a little, but tears still ran down her face.

It didn't matter; she was soaking wet everywhere. She could feel the harsh hands taking off the strait-jacket and weights, removing the mouthpiece. Then, just as she began to really see, she was turned around to face Mr. Zetes.

She was white and wrinkled. Her mouth hurt, she had cramps in her arms and shoulders, and her legs wouldn't support her. She was dripping all over the floor.

"She can't stand up," Joyce said crisply. "Bri, get a chair."

They put her in the chair. Mr. Z looked at her.

Now, what? Kaitlyn asked Gabriel. *I don't think I can scream. Should I just sort of look vacant?*

Try it, he commanded. Now that she could hear real voices, his telepathic voice seemed different. She knew it wasn't sound.

"Can you understand me, Kaitlyn?" Mr. Zetes was asking. "Do you know where you are?"

His expression was avid and eager. Like a connoisseur just about to take the first sip of wine, stopping to inhale the bouquet. If he thought she was crazy enough, he'd say, "Ahhh."

Kaitlyn tried to look mad. She gazed at him, doing her version of the human pupa stare. She wondered if she should try to say, "Muh-muh-muh"—but she was afraid she would do it wrong. Instead, she tried to smile the way Sasha had.

She saw in an instant that it wasn't any good. Mr. Z was an expert on insane people—he collected them. His piercing eyes widened and then narrowed as he looked at her. Kaitlyn would have sworn she could see a red spark somewhere in their depths.

Then his white brows drew together over his aquiline nose and his mouth made a bitter, scornful line. He planted his gold-headed cane on the ground and stood tall, like some patriarch from the Bible. Except that he looked instead like *El Diablo, El Gato,* Satan.

"It's failed," he said. He looked at Joyce. "Why?"

"I don't know. I have no idea." Even Kaitlyn could hear the relief in the shaky voice. Joyce's hand on Kaitlyn's back pressed gently, out of Mr. Z's sight.

"This girl tried to destroy us. Not once. Time and again." Mr. Z's voice was shaking, too—with repressed anger.

Joyce straightened. "I had nothing to do with it, Emmanuel. I don't know how she came through like this. But now that she has—"

Mr. Z's face had been undergoing a struggle—one instant molded by satanic fury, the next smoothing as it was suppressed. Almost like Claymation, Kaitlyn thought. But now he had himself under control. His lips curved in a smile of grim delight.

"Now that she has, we'll just have to try the other

solution," he told Joyce. "The crystal will take care of her."

Kaitlyn felt a falling in her stomach. She looked at Gabriel, who was standing with Renny and Jackal Mac and Lydia, all in a row behind Mr. Z. And at that instant she heard:

Kaitlyn? Kaitlyn, this is Rob. Am I in range yet?

Rob! Oh, thank God, Rob, you're early, thank God.

She felt the flash of Gabriel's response as well. Desperate relief.

Rob, where are you? Kaitlyn demanded.

At the end of the block. We were worried you might be in trouble.

We are! Rob, you'd better hurry.

At the same time Gabriel was saying, *If you can make a distraction, I can try to get Kait out.*

Then Kaitlyn snapped to the real world. Frost had darted forward and grabbed her hand, wrapping her silver-nailed fingers around it.

"Mr. Zetes, I know how she did it!" Frost shrieked, her voice thin and sharp with spite. "She's talking to them! She was talking to them just now, and she's scared they'll get caught because they're coming right here!"

Kaitlyn jerked her hand away as if she'd touched a live coal. Red fury exploded inside her and she kept pulling her hand back to get distance, and then she slapped Frost's cheek as hard as she could.

But Gabriel kept his head. She could hear him yelling a warning to Rob. *Stay where you are! They just found out about you! Don't come near the house!*

"Quickly," Mr. Z said, and his smile was more delighted than ever. He rolled the words in his mouth as if enjoying them. "John, Laurie, Paul—help

Kaitlyn downstairs, please. Everyone else follow. Hurry now. This should be very interesting."

Kaitlyn tried to fight Mac and Frost and Renny, but her limbs were too weak. She was more of a hindrance by just being limp.

Gabriel didn't fight, either—probably too many of them, Kaitlyn thought. But she didn't understand why he seemed to be hanging back, the last one down the stairs to the hidden room. She tried to get a look at him as they carried her down, but she couldn't see.

"I want to kill him myself!" Gabriel shouted from the floor above. Kaitlyn felt the pang of a new terror: What if the crystal had driven Gabriel crazy like the others? And it was just showing up now?

Gabriel—

He wouldn't answer her. Because Frost was touching her? She didn't know.

"Come down!" Mr. Zetes shouted as he punched in the combination to the office.

Kaitlyn didn't want to go in there. Did not. She struggled with fresh strength as they carried her through the door.

Then the smell and the psychic feel of the human pupae struck her and she went limp.

They carried her past the crystal to the only piece of furniture in the room, a chair. Everyone else was crowding in. Mr. Z was herding them, gesturing them to pack themselves more tightly. Like somebody trying to fit more people into an elevator. Gabriel was the last. He stepped back to join the others who were lining the walls.

Then Mr. Zetes backed up. He stood, leaning both hands on his cane, looking at the doorway with anticipation.

"They won't come," Kaitlyn told him. Her voice

was earnest; she just wished it was steady. "I warned them and they're too smart to come when they know you're waiting."

Mr. Zetes smiled. "Do you hear that, my dear? The kitchen door breaking."

Rob? Are you in the house? Rob, listen to me—don't do it. Stay away! Stay away!

But the imperious tone that had worked with him in the gym did nothing now.

This is my choice, Kaitlyn, Rob said. And Kaitlyn heard footsteps on the stairs.

15

Rob, go back!" Kaitlyn screamed aloud.

Rob came in. He was flushed and windblown, his hair a golden lion's mane, his eyes full of all the light of the sky. He had run down the stairs, but he took the step into the room calmly, face alert and purposeful, assessing his chances. Looking for Kaitlyn and the way to get her out.

"Leave," Kaitlyn whispered.

Anna and Lewis were right behind Rob. Stepping over the threshold and into the trap. Behind them was a girl Kaitlyn recognized vaguely . . . yellow curls and tilted eyes . . . of course, it was Tamsin.

"A visitor from the Fellowship!" Mr. Zetes said. "We are greatly honored." He actually bowed over his cane.

He didn't move to shut the door. He didn't have to. Once they were all in, he nudged Parté King with his foot, not quite a kick.

Kaitlyn felt power swelling out to hold the new arrivals in the room. As if a fence had been stretched across the open doorway. Rob stared at the lolling creatures on the floor, his face going pale under his tan, the light in his eyes fading with shock.

And even as he stared, he was caught, his movements dragged into slow motion. So were the others. Like flies in flypaper, Kaitlyn thought. Gnats in a web.

"What did you do to them?" Rob whispered, looking slowly from Sasha to Mr. Zetes.

"The unfortunate pilot study," Mr. Zetes said blandly. "Don't look so alarmed. You'll find it isn't so bad after a while."

"Muhhh," said Sasha.

Rob tried to move toward Mr. Zetes—Kaitlyn saw the determination in his face, saw his muscles cord as he strained. But Sasha and Parté King were watching him. Their power surged up to hold Rob tighter. Kaitlyn could *feel* it happening as well as see it. Rob stopped fighting and stood panting.

"You should have stayed away, Rob," Joyce said, in a voice that seemed on the edge of tears. "I wish you had; I really do."

Rob didn't glance at her. He looked at Kaitlyn.

I'm sorry, Kait. I blew it.

Kaitlyn felt wetness spill from her eyes. *I'm the one who's sorry. It's my fault we're all here.* She looked at Tamsin, wondering if there was any hope. The people of the Fellowship were born to a psychic race, they had all sorts of ancient knowledge. Was there some weapon . . . ?

But Tamsin's face undeceived her. Tamsin was gazing mutely at the two creatures on the floor, her lips parted with pity and helpless sorrow. She didn't even seem to recognize the possibility of fighting.

Aspect, Kaitlyn thought. The philosophy of the Fellowship. Nonviolence, passive resistance.

It wasn't going to get Tamsin very far here.

"I didn't realize that this morning would be so productive," Mr. Zetes said happily. He was doing everything but rubbing his hands, gloating. "These last two days have been splendid—just splendid. And now we'll finish up."

He took a step toward Rob, unaffected by the dragging power of the human pupae.

"I'm going to leave you down here to get acquainted with my former students," he said. "I think in a short time you'll all be on the same level of communication —especially if I tie you in actual contact with the crystal. Contact is quite painful, especially in large doses in the beginning. But of course you know that already."

"We can't just disappear," Anna said. "Our parents will come looking. My parents know about you already. They'll find out what you've done and then they'll kill you."

"In other words, I won't get away with it," Mr. Zetes translated, still bland. "Go on, say it, my dear; I don't mind the cliché. But the fact is that I *will* get away with it. Literally, you see. I have many different residences across the country; even abroad. And the crystal isn't as much of an encumbrance as you might think. I've already brought it to the United States from a very far place." He looked at Tamsin as if this were a shared joke.

She didn't respond. He shrugged very slightly and went on. "So, you see, I can take my crystal and my students wherever I go—and that's all I need. I'll leave you here, of course. In your parents' care."

He gave his terrible smile.

Kaitlyn was proud of her mind-mates. They stood

in the doorway, snarled with invisible thread, but none of them broke down or showed any fear. Anna's head was high on her slim neck, her dark eyes proud and self-contained. Lewis stood squarely, fists clenched, his round face stern and unreadable. Rob looked like a young and angry angel.

I love you, Kaitlyn told them. *I love you and I'm so proud of you.*

A voice broke into her admiration.

"I won't go with you! I'll stay here with them," Lydia said passionately.

Mr. Zetes frowned just a little. "Don't be ridiculous."

"I won't go! I hate what you're doing. I hate *you!*" Lydia's elbows were at her sides, fists held shaking near her shoulders. "I don't care if you win this time; I don't care what happens to me; I don't care, I don't *care—*"

"Be quiet!" Mr. Zetes said brutally. Lydia was quiet. But she shook her head, dark hair flying from side to side.

"You'll do as you're told," Mr. Zetes said. "Or you *will* be left here, and I don't think you'll like that." He looked at Joyce, his pleasure in the morning obviously spoiled. "All right," he said abruptly. "Let's finish, so we can get to breakfast. Take those chains off the boys and bring them over here."

Kaitlyn's eyes went to the chains on Parté King and Sasha. They had one on each ankle. Which meant one for her, Rob, Anna, and Lewis each. Tamsin probably wouldn't try to fight.

Then Kaitlyn looked up, because something was wrong. Joyce wasn't moving to obey Mr. Zetes. She was shaking her head.

"I'm not asking you to do it, I'm telling you. Joyce!"

Joyce shook her head again, slowly and decisively, her aquamarine eyes on Mr. Z's face.

"Good for you, Joyce," Kaitlyn said. To Mr. Zetes, she said, "Can't you see? They're all turning against you. It's going to keep happening, too. You can't win."

Mr. Zetes had gone purple.

"Disobedience! Disobedience and insubordination!" he shouted. "Is there anyone here who still understands loyalty?" The piercing eyes flashed around the room. Bri and Renny looked away from him: Bri glowering, Renny with his shoulders angrily hunched. They were both shaking their heads slowly.

Mr. Z's gaze settled on Jackal Mac. "John! Take the key from Joyce and remove those chains immediately!"

Jackal Mac obeyed. He started to feel all over Joyce's pockets for the key, but she slapped his hand away and pulled it out, slowly, staring at Mr. Zetes all the while.

Shambling to the center of the room, Mac unlocked the chains from Sasha.

"Give them to me," Mr. Zetes said impatiently. "Then remove the others."

When Mac did, Mr. Z looked at Rob. Kaitlyn could see that he was fighting to regain his smiling malevolence. But he couldn't do it. He was an angry old man taking revenge.

"Go ahead and struggle," he told Rob. "You won't be able to move. And when I have you chained, these boys on the floor will move you step by step until you touch the crystal. The great crystal, the last of the ancient firestones. Go ahead, take a look at it."

He gestured at the obscene thing towering in the middle of the floor, the crystal that shone with its own milky impure light. The machine of death waiting for them all.

"The moment you touch it, your mind will start to burn," Mr. Zetes went on with some of his old fervor. "In a matter of hours it will burn *out*. Like a gutted house. Your powers will remain, but *you* will not." Kneeling, he brought the chain to Rob's ankle. "And now . . ."

"I don't think so," Gabriel said.

While Mr. Zetes had been talking to Rob, while the human pupae were busy keeping Rob tightly controlled for the chaining, while Jackal Mac was unlocking the other chains, Gabriel had been inching forward. Kaitlyn had seen it, but hadn't known what he could do. He was empty-handed. The pupae would stop any kind of a fight.

But as Gabriel spoke, she heard a swishing *snick*. The sound she'd heard in Marisol's room and on Ivy Street, when his spring-loaded knife snapped out of his sleeve.

Only this time it wasn't a knife.

He was holding the crystal shard by its thick end, holding it underhanded, like a sword ready to thrust up. Its tip was only a foot or so from the giant crystal in the center of the room.

Now Kaitlyn understood why he had been the last one downstairs. He'd been in Joyce's room, getting the shard.

"Don't close that chain," Gabriel said. "Or I'll put it on the crystal."

Kaitlyn heard a metallic click and knew that Mr. Z had done it anyway. He straightened up to look at Gabriel. He was alarmed but not panicked, Kaitlyn thought.

"Now, Gabriel," he said, and moved a little toward him.

Just a little. Gabriel stiffened. The tip of the shard quivered. Kaitlyn could see it reaching for one of the outgrowths of the crystal, like a stalactite and a stalagmite trying to kiss.

"Stay there!"

Mr. Z stopped.

"Now," Gabriel said. "Everyone who doesn't want to die, step back."

At the same time, Mr. Z was kicking the human pupae. "Stop him! Push him back against the wall."

Parté King, the cricketlike one, rolled over on his side to look at Gabriel. Sasha turned his swollen white head. They were both smiling their face-splitting grins.

Kaitlyn felt the power surge up again, sweeping around Gabriel like sticky running tree sap around a fly, turning to amber to hold him. She saw Gabriel start to lunge forward, then freeze in place, the tip of the shard only inches from a jagged outgrowth.

Her throat swelled, and then she was shouting. "Come on! Everybody! If we all move at once— maybe they can't hold us."

She stood, heard Mr. Z yell, and felt the drag of air. She fought it, shouting, "Get to the shard! Somebody get to the shard!"

Then it seemed everyone was either trying to move, or trying to stop someone from moving. Bri was trying to move. Her glower had turned to a look of grim resolve, and Kaitlyn realized she'd finally decided which side she was on. Frost was stopping her, blocking her like a basketball guard. Renny was trying to move. Jackal Mac had abandoned the chains and was grappling with him in slow motion.

Rob and Anna and Lewis were all struggling to get to Gabriel, mostly with their feet stuck to the floor, but occasionally managing a step. Even Tamsin was trying. Mr. Z was turning round and round among them, raising his cane, shouting. He couldn't deal with them all at once.

Then Kaitlyn saw that Lydia was free and moving —slowly but steadily—toward Gabriel and the shard.

"Joyce!" Mr. Zetes shouted. "Stop her! She's right beside you! Stop her!"

But Joyce shook her head. "It's time it was over, Emmanuel," she said. In an instant, she and Lydia were caught in the sticky air, too. Lydia still struggled on desperately.

"Hold them!" Mr. Zetes shouted, and began beating Sasha and Parté King with his cane. "Hold them all! Hold them all!"

Kaitlyn heard the savage swishing sound of the cane, and the dull thud of the blows. She saw Gabriel's face tighten, saw it go grim with purpose. The shard quivered, moved an inch toward the crystal.

"Gabriel," Mr. Zetes said. "Think of all your ambitions. You wanted to go to the top. Have everything good. Money, power, position—all the things in life you deserve."

Gabriel was panting, sweat trickling down his temples.

"Recognition of your superiority—you'll never have any of it without me," Mr. Z went on frantically. "What about all that, Gabriel? Everything you always wanted?"

Gabriel lifted his head just enough to look Mr. Z in the eye. "The hell with it."

Then he gritted his teeth and the shard moved again.

Mr. Zetes lost control.

He began to scream, shrill and piercing, and to beat Sasha again. "Stop him! Stop him! Stop him!"

Sasha's voice rose, too, for the first time since Kaitlyn had seen him. "Muh-muh! *Muhhhh! Muhhhh! Moooootheeerrrr!*"

Kaitlyn screamed herself then. She was crying wildly, fighting the air.

Then suddenly the drag disappeared. The air was air again. Everything that happened next happened in an instant, so that Kaitlyn's mind took it in like a still photograph, receiving the impressions before she could really process them.

She was moving freely. Sasha had turned to look at Mr. Zetes. She could see Sasha's face, not white anymore, but red with the fury of a squalling infant. And then Mr. Zetes was flying toward the crystal, *flying,* as if a giant hand had thrown him. He smashed into it, into its heavy solidity and sword-sharp outcrops at the same instant that Gabriel thrust the shard forward like a rapier.

It all happened at once. Although Kaitlyn's body was free there was no time to *do* anything, only time for one thought, sent out to her mind-mates as she saw the shard stab toward the crystal. With Gabriel still holding it—

Protect Gabriel! Put your thoughts—around him—

The words weren't very clear, but her intent was. She felt everyone in the web, Rob, Lewis, and Anna, joining with her to help shield Gabriel's mind from the destruction.

Mr. Z's high, keening wail came at the same instant, just as the shard made contact with one translucent facet of the crystal.

And then—

There were all sorts of sounds woven together in the great crashing that came next. There was the sound of an axe crashing through glass, and the sound of a sonic boom that rattled the windows. There was the rushing sound of a freight train passing by very close. There was a metallic sound like all the pots and pans in a kitchen falling to a tile floor at once. There was the rumble of thunder and the cracking of ice on a lake. There was a high, thin sound like the screaming of gulls—or maybe that was Mr. Zetes.

And through all the other sounds, underneath them, Kaitlyn thought she could hear music—the kind of music you think you hear when water is crashing through copper pipes.

There was light, too. The kind of light you expect to see just before a mushroom-shaped cloud. Kaitlyn's eyes squeezed shut automatically, and her hand flew up to protect her face, but she saw it through her eyelids.

Colors that her pastels and ink bottles had never prepared her for. Aureolin yellow with a brightness off the scales. Dragon's blood crimson spreading into tongues of lava pink fire. Ultraviolet silvery blue.

They burst like fireworks, sweeping to the edges of her vision, overlapping each other, bright explosion after bright explosion.

And then they stopped. Kaitlyn saw rainbow after-images, beautiful fiery lattices printed on her eyelids.

Very cautiously she opened her eyes, lifting her hand away from her face.

A cobalt green stain still colored her vision, but she could see again. The great milky crystal was dust on the ground, glassy dust in the shape of a giant stone plant, or a Christmas tree ornament. The largest bits left were pebble size.

Mr. Zetes, who had been touching the crystal at the moment it shattered, was gone. Just gone. Nothing left but the gold-topped cane that had fallen from his hand.

Sasha and Parté King were lying still. Their faces were frozen into a look of empty astonishment—not peaceful, but not anguished, either. In her heart, Kaitlyn was sorry she'd called them the human pupae. They had been human beings.

Everyone else was standing pretty much where they had been before the crash. They were all lifting their heads or lowering their hands, staring.

"It's over," Lewis whispered finally. "We did it. It's over."

Kaitlyn was beginning to realize the same thing. Bri and Renny were gazing around them like sleepwalkers who'd just woken up. Free of the influence of the crystal at last, Kait thought. She looked at Gabriel. He was looking at his hand which had held the shard. The palm was pink, as if he'd been lightly burned.

"Did the shard go, too?" Kaitlyn asked.

He turned his gray eyes on her, as if startled to hear a voice. Then he looked back at his hand again.

"Yes," he said, blinking. "When the crystal did. It felt—I can't explain it. It was like lightning in my hand. I felt the power go *through* it. And the power—it felt like Timon. Like Timon and Mereniang and LeShan—all of them. It was as if they were in there, rushing out." He looked up again, almost furtively. "I guess that sounds crazy."

"No, it doesn't," Rob said, his voice strong. "It sounds right. I believe you."

Gabriel looked at him, just a look. But after that he held his head up, and the startled, furtive expression was gone.

Kaitlyn felt something like carbonated water begin to bubble in her veins. "We did it," she said. She looked at each of her mind-mates, and at Lydia, and suddenly she needed to shout. "You guys, we did it!"

"I said that already," Lewis said with force.

And then it was like a roller coaster gathering speed. Everybody seemed to feel the need to say it, and then to yell it, and then to yell louder to be heard over the other yells. People began to tell one another and then to hug one another or pound one another on the back to drive the point home. Kaitlyn found herself shaking Lydia and kissing Gabriel. Rob, somehow unchained, was wringing Anna's long braids.

Bri and Renny were part of the celebration, punching each other and whooping with gathering intensity. Joyce was crying, clutching with one hand at Kaitlyn's back and whispering something Kait couldn't hear. Lydia was a full member of the winning team, being socked in the arm over and over by Lewis.

But three people weren't. Tamsin knelt by the two dead boys on the floor. Her tilted eyes were wet as she gently closed their eyelids.

And Frost and Jackal Mac were stiff as statues, watching the wild release of energy around them with frightened, hostile eyes. Kaitlyn saw them and raised her arms to Frost.

"Come on," she said. "Don't worry; be happy. Let's all try to deal with each other, okay?"

It wasn't the warmest invitation, maybe, but Kaitlyn thought that under the circumstances it was pretty generous. But Frost's pale blue eyes flashed. Jackal Mac's face turned ugly.

They looked at each other, then with one accord they rushed for the door.

Kaitlyn was too surprised to try to stop them, and

by the time she recovered, she wasn't sure she wanted to. The yelling and cheering had died out, and she looked at Rob, who had taken half a step toward the door.

"I think we should just let them go," she said.

He glanced back, then nodded slowly. Gabriel and Lewis settled back reluctantly. Kaitlyn could hear running footsteps up above, then the bang of a door.

Then, silence. In the stillness, Joyce's whispering could be heard.

"I'm so sorry. I'm so sorry for everything."

Kaitlyn turned.

Joyce's aquamarine eyes were red-rimmed. Her face was shiny with tears and perspiration, her normally sleek blond hair ruffled like a baby chick's. Her pink sweat clothes looked damp and bedraggled.

She also looked like a sleepwalker who has just woken up.

"I'm so sorry," she whispered. "The things I've done. The terrible things. I . . . I . . ."

Kaitlyn looked at her helplessly. Then she said, "Tamsin!"

The head with the clustered yellow curls lifted. Tamsin saw Joyce and got up. She looked into Joyce's face, then she took Joyce by the elbow and led her toward the open door.

"The firestones can cast a powerful spell," Kait heard her saying softly. "Their influence can be very strong—and recovery can take a long time. . . ."

Kaitlyn was satisfied. Although Tamsin looked younger than Joyce, there was a sort of ageless wisdom and understanding about her. Joyce was listening as they disappeared.

Kait turned back to find her mind-mates grinning at her.

Good job, Lewis said, and Anna said, *I hope she's okay.*

Bri and Renny were smiling, too. The atmosphere of wild jubilation had quieted, but a kind of dizzy glow remained.

"Let's go upstairs," Rob said, taking Kaitlyn's hand.

"Yes, I'd better change." Kaitlyn glanced down at the bathing suit and grinned wryly. "And I'm sure there are things to take care of—God, the police, I guess. We're going to have to explain all this somehow."

"I wanna get out of here before *that,*" Bri said.

Kaitlyn looked behind her, held out her free hand to Gabriel. "Come on, you . . . *hero.* I want to tell you what I think of you."

"So do I," Rob said, golden eyes warm.

Gabriel looked at Kaitlyn's fingers intertwined with Rob's. He smiled, but Kaitlyn couldn't feel his happiness in the web anymore.

"I'm glad you have her back safe again," he said to Rob. He was saying two things with that, Kaitlyn realized.

Suddenly, some of the dizzy glow faded. "Please come up with us," she said to Gabriel, and he nodded, smiling politely, like a stranger.

16

So you're not a psychic vampire anymore," Lewis said to Gabriel as they reached the dining room. "I mean, nobody is anymore, right? The Fellowship said if the crystal was destroyed, you'd be cured."

Kaitlyn realized that he was chattering deliberately, filling the silence, trying to help in the only way he could. Gabriel smiled at him, wanly grateful, but Kaitlyn could see the pain behind those gray eyes.

She herself knew that she should be going upstairs, but she couldn't seem to make herself leave. She had never imagined that a person could go from feeling so gloriously happy to so wretchedly miserable in such an appallingly short time.

Wretched, and frightened, and sick with pain. I'm being torn in two, she thought, standing in the sunlit dining room and holding Rob's hand even tighter. I'll never be whole again; I'll never be all right. Oh, God, *please,* please tell me what to do.

She pulled her hand away from Rob, because even

200

her shields couldn't contain the pain. She didn't want him to know.

Anna slipped a jacket over her shoulders and gave Kaitlyn's hand a squeeze. Kaitlyn looked at her gratefully, unable to speak.

Rob was looking a bit lost. "Well—is anybody hurt?" he said, glancing around. "Kaitlyn—?"

"I'm fine. Gabriel's hand, though . . ."

Gabriel, who had just sat down, looked up sharply. "It's all right. Just a little burn." He had been pushing his sweater sleeve off his forearm, scratching under it absently, but now he pulled it down again.

"Let me see. No, I said, *let me see.*" Rob clamped Gabriel's left arm with an unbreakable grip.

"No, leave it alone. It's the other hand!" Gabriel's tone was almost as harsh as it had been in the old days, but Kaitlyn detected a note almost of panic underneath.

"But I feel something here. Stop fighting and hold still!" Rob's voice was equally annoyed. He wrestled the sleeve up by main force—and then stared.

Gabriel's pale forearm was covered with ghastly marks. Angry red cuts, their lips curling open and beginning to bleed again with the rough handling. Burns that were turning brown at the edges and still blistered in the middle. They ran all the way from wrist to elbow.

Kaitlyn felt giddy.

"What happened?" Rob said, with terrible quietness. "Who did this to you?" He lifted clear golden eyes to Gabriel's face, waiting.

"Nobody." Gabriel looked angry, but somehow relieved, too. "It just—happened. It happened when the crystal broke."

There was a silence, a heaviness in the web. Lewis frowned, Anna's lips pulled in at the corners. Bri and Renny had backed off, as if recognizing somehow this wasn't their business. Rob was looking at Gabriel hard.

Kaitlyn was trying to blink dancing spots away. She felt she should know what had happened to Gabriel. She should know, if she could only *think.* . . .

"Well, relax," Rob said finally, evenly. "I can make it stop hurting so much. Make it heal faster."

He put one hand on Gabriel's arm above the elbow and held Gabriel's palm with the other. Kaitlyn could see him feeling with his fingers for transfer points. Gabriel sat, uncharacteristically docile and obedient.

Rob's thumb pressed into Gabriel's palm and he shut his eyes. Through the web, Kaitlyn could feel what he was doing. Sending healing energy through the wounded limb, stimulating Gabriel's own energy to flow, as well. Golden sparks traveling down Gabriel's veins, golden mist enveloping the forearm. Kaitlyn felt warmth, and felt Gabriel relaxing as the pain eased, his muscles unclenching.

With relaxation, barriers go down. Kaitlyn knew that, and she knew that Rob's healing brought him closer to people. In a minute, she knew that he was doing something else to Gabriel. Probing his mind, looking for something.

Hey! Gabriel tried to jerk his arm out of the steely grip, head lifting, face furious. But it was too late.

They stared at each other a long moment, gray eyes and gold locked as they always had been when the two of them did battle. Locked for endless, time-stretching seconds.

Then Rob's face changed and he settled back on his heels.

Gabriel held his hurt arm to his chest protectively, his own expression defensive and defiant.

"You did those to your own self," Rob said flatly, calmly. Still looking Gabriel in the eyes. "To . . . stay in contact with Kaitlyn." He said the words as if he weren't exactly sure of their meaning. "They were doing something to her and you had to talk to her over a long range. So you thought pain would help you call louder."

Gabriel said nothing, but Kaitlyn felt the truth of it. That was what he'd been concealing when he talked to her in the isolation tank. When he gave her his best memories. She'd felt fatigue and some kind of pain, but he'd shielded most of it from her.

"You used somebody's cigar and a piece of broken glass," Rob said, with growing confidence. "And then later you poked at the sores some more to keep awake."

Yes, Kaitlyn thought, feeling it with Rob in the web. She could tell he didn't exactly understand what the situation was, but that he was sure about one thing.

"You love her, don't you?" he said to Gabriel.

Gabriel finally seemed able to break their locked stare. He looked away, at the carpet. His face was bleak.

"Yes," he said.

"More than anything," Rob persisted. "You'd crawl on your belly over broken glass for her. Easy."

"Yes, damn you," Gabriel said. "Happy now?"

Rob looked at Kaitlyn.

Kaitlyn's head was swimming, her body racked in so many different directions that she stood still. She couldn't seem to put a coherent thought together. But on top of everything else, holding her precariously in one piece, was the thought that she mustn't hurt Rob.

She loved him too much to hurt him. And she knew that Gabriel's eyes on her were saying the same thing.

She now knew that it *was* possible to love two people at once—because you could love them in different ways. The love she felt for Rob now was a burning tenderness, a knowledge that he was the one who'd taught her it was *possible* to love, who had melted the ice of her heart. It was strong and gentle and steady, full of admiration and the intimacy of shared likes and dislikes. It was golden and warm like a summer afternoon.

And if it wasn't the passion and desperate depth of feeling she had for Gabriel, she never wanted Rob to know.

But as Rob looked at her, gazing with those clear eyes full of light, she realized that her shields were in tatters around her. She had been awake for two days and in agony or terror for nearly as long. She didn't have anything *left* to shield with.

And she could see, she could feel, that he was seeing right inside her. Rob knew.

"Why didn't you tell me?" he asked her after a small eternity.

"I didn't—I didn't feel that way—until—so many things have happened . . ." Kaitlyn faltered. Of all things, she wanted to make Rob all right. Although now she saw that her love for him must have been changing for a long time, gradually, she didn't know how to explain that. "It's probably just—I'll get over it. In a little while . . ."

"Not that, you won't," Rob said. "Neither of you. I mean, I sure hope you don't." He sounded as incoherent as Kaitlyn felt, and he kept swallowing. But he went on doggedly, "Kait, I love you. You know I do. But this isn't something I can compete with." He stepped back. "I'm not blind. You two belong together."

He looked . . . distressed, Kaitlyn realized vaguely. Distressed, but not devastated. Not ruined for life. There was so much more to Rob.

And, as she watched, Anna moved up and put her hand on his back from behind. Kaitlyn looked at her over Rob's shoulder.

Anna smiled tremulously. Her dark eyes were wet but glowing somewhere down inside.

Suddenly a vast, rushing lightness filled Kaitlyn. As if a huge and heavy weight had been taken off her chest. She stared at Anna, and at the way Rob unconsciously was leaning back against Anna's arm. And the effervescent bubbles lifted her skyward.

I just had a precognition, she told Anna silently, a stream of unspoken love and joy. *You will be very happy. Your best friend says to go for it.*

Anna's face was bright, as if someone had set a candle behind it. *You're giving me permission?*

I'm giving you an order!

Lewis laughed out loud. Then he said, "Didn't somebody say something about cleaning up? And how about some food?"

Bri and Renny and Lydia seemed to recognize that as a signal. They followed him as he started for the kitchen. Anna tugged at Rob's arm, gently, to bring him, too.

Rob looked back, once.

I'm glad, he told Gabriel, and Kaitlyn could hear the truth in it. *I mean, it hurts, but I'm glad for you. Take care of her.*

Then he was gone.

Slowly, Kaitlyn turned to Gabriel.

It had occurred to her at the last minute that

nobody had really asked him. Maybe, even if he loved her, he'd prefer that the feeling go away. Maybe he didn't want her now that everybody had had a hand in the procedure.

But Gabriel was looking at her now, and she could see his eyes.

She had seen those eyes dark with brooding anger and cold as ice, she'd seen his gaze veiled like a spiderweb and shattering like agate under pressure. But she'd never seen them as they were now. Full of wondering joy and disbelief, and an almost frightened awe.

Gabriel was trying to smile, but the expression kept breaking apart. He was looking at her as if he hadn't seen her for years and years of searching, and had just now walked into a room and come upon her unexpectedly. As if he wanted to look at every part of her, now that he could do it honestly.

Kaitlyn remembered the things he'd given her, the sun-flooded afternoons, and the cool healing ocean waves, and the music he'd written. He'd given her everything that was best in him, everything he was.

She wanted to give him the same back again.

I don't know how you can love me. The words came softly, as if he were thinking them to himself. *You've seen what I am.*

That's why I do love you, Kaitlyn told him. *I hope you'll still love me when you see what I am.*

"I know what you are, Kait. Everything beautiful and brave and gallant and . . ." He stopped as if his throat had closed. "Everything that makes me want to be better for you. That makes me sorry I'm such a stupid mess. . . ."

You looked like a knight with the shard, Kaitlyn said, moving toward him.

"Really?" He laughed shakily.

My knight. And I never said thank you.

She was almost touching him, now. Looking up into his eyes. What she could feel in him was something she'd only felt before when she gave him her life energy. Childlike, marveling joy. Trust and vulnerability. And such love . . .

Then she was in his arms and they weren't separate beings any longer. Their minds were together, sharing thoughts, sharing a happiness beyond thought. Sharing everything.

She never even knew whether he kissed her.

It seemed a very long time later, but the sunbeams falling across the dining room had hardly moved. Kaitlyn had her head on Gabriel's shoulder. She was so full of peace—peace and light and hope for everything. Even the nagging hole in the universe where LeShan had been was filled with light. She hoped that, somehow, he knew what had happened today and was satisfied.

"God make me worthy of you. Fast," Gabriel said. It was something like a command.

Kaitlyn smiled. His arms were tight around her, a feeling she never wanted to lose. But they were no longer outside time, and she could hear banging and shouting laughter from upstairs.

"I guess we'd better see what's going on," she said.

Very slowly, most reluctantly, he let her go, only keeping her hand in his. They walked around the corner to the stairs.

Lydia, though, was just coming down. Bri and Renny were behind her. They'd obviously been going through closets; each had a full cardboard box and at least one bag or suitcase.

"We don't know exactly what we'll need there," Lydia told Kaitlyn. Her green eyes looked out almost shyly from behind her heavy shock of dark hair.

"Go where?" Kaitlyn asked.

"You didn't hear? Oh, I guess not." Lydia headed for the front lab, with Bri and Renny following. Kaitlyn and Gabriel followed *them*.

"Joyce is going with Tamsin back to the Fellowship," Lydia said, dumping her box on a desk. "Ouch. That was heavy."

"Going back with Tamsin?"

"Yup," Bri said. "And we're going with her."

Kaitlyn stared. Renny was nodding, pushing up his glasses with an index finger.

"Tamsin says it'll help Joyce heal from the influence of the crystal," Lydia said. "And Bri and Renny, too. Oh, here they are."

Joyce and Tamsin came in from the kitchen. Joyce's hair was smoothed again, and her lips had stopped trembling. She seemed to be hanging on Tamsin's every word.

"We'd be glad to have you," Tamsin was saying. "And we can help the children develop and control their powers. Even Lydia . . ."

"I don't have any powers," Lydia said.

Tamsin smiled at her. "You're of the old race. We'll see."

Kaitlyn noticed the sunlight change and realized that Rob was in the kitchen doorway. Lewis and Anna were right behind him, but Anna was closer.

Rob smiled at her, and it was a real smile, with his own gladness and optimism behind it. "Tamsin's been telling us about their place on the new island," he said. "They've got it pretty rough, but they're working on it. It's been hard with Mereniang gone, and now that LeShan is dead . . ." He shook his head, but his eyes were gleaming as if he saw a challenge.

"Rob! Are you telling me—do you want to go, too?"

"Well, I was thinking about it. They're going to need help."

"And leadership," Tamsin said, quietly, without sounding ashamed. "Innovation, new ideas—they don't come easily to us."

Rob nodded. "You help us and we help you. A fair exchange."

And the great task Rob's been looking for, Kaitlyn thought, somewhat giddy with the suddenness of it. Not saving the world, maybe, but fixing a little part of it.

She didn't know what to say. She was remembering Canada, the lush beauty of the rain forest, the open vastness of the sky. The wild blue ocean.

"Of course, the rest of you children can stay here," Joyce was saying. "Not at the Institute—that will be closed for good. But I think I could arrange for you to have your scholarships after all. Mr. Zetes had the money put aside in a special account; he had to, for the lawyers."

Yes, that was the sensible thing to do. School and then college. Her father would want that. And Gabriel was a city boy. Kaitlyn's fingers tightened on his— and then she felt his thought.

Well, we could just take a vacation, couldn't we? he asked. His gray eyes were sparkling.

Happiness flooded Kaitlyn to her fingertips.

We could—yes, we could, she told Rob and Anna and Lewis. *We could make up the time at school next year. And meanwhile, it would be very educational. . . .*

And we wouldn't break the web, Rob said, and she

could feel his joy, too. He and Gabriel were smiling at each other.

Of course, we'll have *to break it someday,* Lewis said quickly. *I mean, we can't go around this way forever.*

Of course not, Anna agreed solemnly, her owl eyes crinkling at the edges.

But just for now . . . Lewis said.

Just for now, they all agreed, together.

Talk was going on around them. Joyce was moving toward the front door, saying, "What's that?" Lydia was rummaging through her box.

"I forgot to show you. Look what I found!" she said to Lewis. She was holding two things: an alarm clock shaped like a cow—and his camera.

"Hey, where did you get that? That's precious!" Lewis said, taking the cow.

"I know. I want you to show me what it does." Lydia smiled at him, her new shy smile, and Lewis beamed back. He reached out and squeezed her arm, just once.

"As soon as we get alone," he said wickedly, "I will."

"Kaitlyn! Rob!" Joyce was calling from the front door in a voice wavering between laughter and tears. "There's someone here to see you, and I don't think you should keep her waiting!"

They all went, Kaitlyn and Gabriel and Rob and Anna, with Lewis and Lydia following, and Tamsin bringing up the rear with Bri and Renny. When Kaitlyn got to the porch she stopped in astonishment.

"Oh . . ." was all she could say. Then she said, "Oh, *Marisol."*

It was Marisol, thin and rather wobbly on her legs, supported on Tony's arm. She was pale, but her tumbled mahogany hair was the same as Kaitlyn remembered, and a smile was trembling on her full lips.

"I came to see the guy who healed me," she said. "And all of you."

"All of them were in it," Tony said proudly. He had a shirt on today, Kaitlyn noticed, and he looked as if someone had just willed him a million dollars.

Kaitlyn hugged Marisol, and then she had to stand back so Rob could do it. And then Lydia was coming forward, and Bri, looking as if they thought Marisol might hate them. But she smiled at them instead, and there were more hugs. Those who couldn't hug Marisol hugged one another.

And Joyce, with her aquamarine eyes on Marisol's face, looked as if healing had already begun.

"We brought you your kitten, too," Tony said to Anna.

"So now everybody's here," Anna said, pressing the kitten to her cheek, then to Rob's.

"Hey, yeah—everybody's here! Wait a minute!" Lewis was running. He was back in a moment. "Everybody, scrunch together by the door. Some of you get down. The rest lean in! Get closer!"

I think we're already about as close as we can get, Gabriel said, and Kaitlyn was surrounded by silent laughter.

"That's it! Hold that smile!" Lewis shouted, and snapped their picture.

ABOUT THE AUTHOR

LISA JANE SMITH is the author of more than twenty books for young adults. She enjoys writing about strong female characters and encouraging girls to read, write, and reach for their dreams. A former teacher, she lives in the Bay area of northern California. Her Archway trilogies include *The Forbidden Game* and *Dark Visions*.

R·L·STINE'S
GHOSTS OF FEAR STREET ®

A MINSTREL® BOOK

Simon & Schuster Mail Order
200 Old Tappan Rd., Old Tappan, N.J. 07675
Please send me the books I have checked above. I am enclosing $_____ (please add
$0.75 to cover the postage and handling for each order. Please add appropriate sales
tax). Send check or money order--no cash or C.O.D.'s please. Allow up to six weeks
for delivery. For purchase over $10.00 you may use VISA: card number, expiration
date and customer signature must be included.

POCKET
B O O K S

Name _____

Address _____

City _____ State/Zip _____

VISA Card # _____ Exp.Date _____

Signature _____ 1180-15

Christopher Pike presents....
a frighteningly fun new series for your younger brothers and sisters!

The Secret Path	53725-3/$3.50
The Howling Ghost	53726-1/$3.50
The Haunted Cave	53727-X/$3.50
Aliens in the Sky	53728-8/$3.99
The Cold People	55064-0/$3.99
The Witch's Revenge	55065-9/$3.99
The Dark Corner	55066-7/$3.99
The Little People	55067-5/$3.99
The Wishing Stone	55068-3/$3.99
The Wicked Cat	55069-1/$3.99
The Deadly Past	55072-1/$3.99
The Hidden Beast	55073-X/$3.99
The Creature in the Teacher	
	00261-9/$3.99
The Evil House	00262-7/$3.99
Invasion of the No-Ones	
	00263-5/$3.99

A MINSTREL® BOOK